"It's obvious that you like being alone, so I apologize for intruding.

"I know I'd hate it if I wanted to be alone and someone tried to die in my front yard, and I had to put them in my bed, and..."

Alicia's voice trailed off. That was the last thing she wanted to think about now—being in this man's bed. She bit her lip as he looked at her, his gaze partially obscured for a moment by his dark hair and narrowed eyes. Then he tucked his hair behind his ear, and she caught the full impact of his direct gaze. "How hot do you like your chili?" he asked. "Boring, interesting or exciting?"

She had a disturbing feeling he could have inserted the word "men" for "chili" and had a valid question for her. And there was no doubt where this man would fit. "Exciting," she murmered.

Dear Reader,

Spring is on its way in at last, but we've got some hot books to keep you warm during the last few chilly days. There's our American Hero title, for example: Ann Williams's *Cold, Cold Heart.* Here's a man who has buried all his feelings, all his hopes and dreams, a man whose job it is to rescue missing children—and who can't get over the tragedy of failure. Into his life comes a woman he can't resist, a woman whose child has been stolen from her, and suddenly he's putting it all on the line all over again. He's back to saving children—and back to dreaming of love. Will his cold heart melt? You take a guess!

Mary Anne Wilson completes her "Sister, Sister" duet with *Two Against the World.* For all of you who loved *Two for the Road,* here's the sequel you've been waiting for. And if you missed the first book, don't worry. You can still order a copy—just don't let Ali's story slip through your hands in the meantime!

The rest of the month is filled with both familiar names—like Maura Seger and Amanda Stevens—and new ones—like Diana Whitney, who makes her Intimate Moments debut, and Dani Criss, who's publishing her very first book. I think you'll enjoy everything we have to offer, as well as everything that will be heading your way in months to come. And speaking of the future, look for some real excitement next month, when Intimate Moments celebrates its tenth anniversary with a can't-miss lineup of books, including Patricia Gardner Evans's long-awaited American Hero title, *Quinn Eisley's War.* Come May, Intimate Moments is definitely *the* place to be.

Yours,
Leslie J. Wainger
Senior Editor and Editorial Coordinator

TWO AGAINST THE WORLD

Mary Anne Wilson

Silhouette® ™
INTIMATE MOMENTS®
Published by Silhouette Books New York
America's Publisher of Contemporary Romance

SILHOUETTE BOOKS
300 East 42nd St., New York, N.Y. 10017

TWO AGAINST THE WORLD

Copyright © 1993 by Mary Anne Wilson

All rights reserved. Except for use in any review, the reproduction or utilization of this work in whole or in part in any form by any electronic, mechanical or other means, now known or hereafter invented, including xerography, photocopying and recording, or in any information storage or retrieval system, is forbidden without the permission of the publisher, Silhouette Books, 300 E. 42nd St., New York, N.Y. 10017

ISBN: 0-373-07489-1

First Silhouette Books printing April 1993

All the characters in this book have no existence outside the imagination of the author and have no relation whatsoever to anyone bearing the same name or names. They are not even distantly inspired by any individual known or unknown to the author, and all incidents are pure invention.

®: Trademark used under license and registered in the United States Patent and Trademark Office and in other countries.

Printed in the U.S.A.

Books by Mary Anne Wilson

Silhouette Intimate Moments

Hot-Blooded #230
Home Fires #267
Liar's Moon #292
Straight from the Heart #304
Dream Chasers #336
Brady's Law #350
Child of Mine #374
Nowhere To Run #410
Echoes of Roses #438
Two for the Road #472
Two Against the World #489

MARY ANNE WILSON

fell in love with reading at ten years of age when she discovered *Pride and Prejudice*. A year later, she knew she had to be a writer when she found herself writing a new ending for *A Tale of Two Cities*. A true romantic, she had Sydney Carton rescued, and he lived happily ever after.

Though she's a native of Canada, she now lives in California with her husband and three children, a six-toed black cat who believes he's Hungarian and five timid Dobermans, who welcome any and all strangers. And she's writing happy endings for her own books.

**For Pax,
with love**

Prologue

Los Angeles, California—December 29, noon, PST

Déjà vu.

Alicia Sullivan felt as if she had been thrust into the past, condemned to repeat all the mistakes she'd made in her life. She thought she'd changed. In the past months, she'd worked hard at changing—"settling down"; getting a nine-to-five job at Paradise Travels; living with her foster mother, Lydia; and actually considering marriage.

She wasn't drifting anymore. She wasn't living on the edge. She wasn't attracting danger like some human magnet. She'd changed.

Yet here she was, with less than two hours to make her flight out of Los Angeles International to Denver, sitting all alone in an interrogation room of a police station ten blocks from her house. Worst of all, she remembered this room. The beige walls, the brown tiled floors, the wooden table, the hard chairs, and the clock bolted to the wall. She even remembered the odors of staleness and disinfectant in air that was stirred by a temperature control system.

She'd been seventeen, over eleven years ago, and she'd come in here to find her twin, Alison, sitting at this same table. Ali had been furious. She'd agreed to pretend to be Alicia for Grad Night, to take over a date with Brad something-or-other. And the night had ended with Brad drinking, plowing into the back end of a police patrol car and both Alison and him being arrested.

Alicia had known that night that she had to leave, that she couldn't stay in the life that her sister seemed to thrive on. And she'd begun a part of her life where she'd kept on the move. She never looked back—she did just what she wanted, when she wanted, with whom she wanted.

All that had come to a grinding halt fourteen months ago in Las Vegas, Nevada, when she'd met a man named Mick Terrine. Mick had turned out to be the only son of a man who was rumored to be the head of a large crime syndicate, and Mick had followed in his father's footsteps. He'd murdered a man. He'd told Alicia all about it after he'd gotten drunk, and she'd become the only witness against him for the state.

She sat back in the hard wooden chair and pressed her hands flat against the edge of the table. Her nerves were raw, and she had the most horrible feeling of waiting for her doom. That brought an unsteady chuckle from her. Fourteen months ago she wouldn't have doubted the day of doom had come. But not now.

"I said goodbye to Lydia, set off for the airport, and my whole life went crazy," she muttered to herself. First she had seen flashing lights in the rearview mirror, then a uniformed policeman stopped her and told her he'd been sent to pick her up and take her to the station as quickly as possible. No explanations, no reasons given.

" 'Follow me to the station,' he says, and he brings me up here to the interrogation room, tells me someone will be with me soon, then leaves." She exhaled harshly and looked at the wall clock. Noon. "Ten minutes and 'someone' never showed up and I've got an hour and a half to make my flight."

She tipped her chair back on two legs, then sat forward with a thud. She'd had enough. "That's it. I'm not going to sit here and wait for someone to come. I'll go and find out what's going on." She stood, tugging at the hem of the bulky white sweater she was wearing with slim corduroy slacks and calf-high leather boots. Then she flipped her long coppery curls behind her shoulders and grabbed her purse off the table.

But before she could do more than hook the leather strap over her shoulder, the door opened and her sister hurried into the room. The feeling of reliving the past came back with a vengeance, but it was a strangely reversed scene. Alison was rushing into the room this time, and Alicia was the one being held by the police.

Alicia stared at her sister, her mirror image with the same fiery red hair, the same heart-shaped face dominated by wide-set, pure green eyes and the hint of freckles at her small, straight nose. Both were tall at almost five feet ten inches, and leggy.

But where Alicia was almost boyishly slender in the sweater and slacks, Alison was very pregnant. The loose pink tunic she was wearing with black leggings and leather flats showed the swelling of eight months of pregnancy. She'd caught her hair back off her face in a low ponytail, and her makeup was almost nonexistent.

"Ali, how did you know I was here?" Alicia said.

As the door clicked shut behind her, Ali came to the table. "The officer at the desk told me you were in here." Her voice was breathless. "What happened?"

Alicia sank back onto the chair and put her purse where it had been on the table. "I was pulled over by a cop and brought in here like some...some criminal."

"What did you do?"

"Nothing, and I—"

"Were you breaking the law?"

"No, but—" It suddenly struck her that her sister hadn't fully answered her first question. "How did you know I'd been brought in?"

Alison folded her arms across her stomach. "Jack called about fifteen minutes ago and told me to meet him here. He told me you had been picked up."

Jack knew about this? Her brother-in-law worked for the district attorney's office as a prosecutor, and now Alicia knew for sure something really awful was about to happen. And if he was involved in this, it had to be big. *Big.* That single word brought everything into focus. She understood. "Oh, God," she whispered. "George Terrine's going to kill me, isn't he?"

Ali paled, and Alicia buried her face in her hands. Even though every cop in Las Vegas had assured her that Mick's father would forget all about her, she'd lived for fourteen months with the dread that he'd come after her. Even though the police had been sure that the father had had his son cold-bloodedly eliminated to protect the organization, she'd known he would, sooner or later, come after her.

"Alicia, Jack didn't even mention George Terrine."

She dropped her hands to her purse, clenching the leather tightly, and stared at her knuckles turning white. "It's Terrine. I know it is. He's sent someone after me to kill me. Probably Sharp."

"Sharp dropped off the face of the earth. He's probably dead. Jack never mentioned Terrine. He just said you were here, and that I should come here."

"That's why the cop used his siren and made me follow him here. That's why I'm here." She was muttering to herself now, ignoring Ali. "Terrine's coming after me. He hasn't forgotten. I should have never trusted Jack and the police. They were stupid to think that he would just write me off, that he would...would call it a wash." She shook her head. "Jack said since Mick was dead that I never had to testify. That it wasn't my fault. That it was over and done." She stood again, twisting the strap of her purse around her hand. "It's not over. They were wrong. All of them."

"Slow down, Alicia."

She looked at Ali, having almost forgotten her sister was there. "They were dead wrong."

"Alicia, Jack's been keeping track of the old man. He's been in seclusion for months. The rumor is he's ill. He wouldn't even remember who you were anymore."

Alicia hugged her purse to her middle. "Ali, he tried to kill me...you...us. He remembers. He was just biding his time." She started around the table. "And I'm out of here."

"What are you talking about?" Ali demanded.

Alicia stopped, killing the urge to run for the door and keep going until this was all a distant nightmare. "I'm leaving. I'm doing what I should have done back in Las Vegas before everyone talked me out of it. I'll disappear. I'll go away and vanish."

"No, you can't. You just got back."

Alicia hated the look of pain on her sister's face, but it was better than having some animal like Terrine's right-hand man, Sharp, coming after her and having Ali caught in the middle. "I have to, Ali. I have to."

Ali held up both hands palm out. "All right, but at least wait for Jack to get here. Let him explain so you know what you're up against. He can get you protection, or maybe he's got a place you can go."

Alicia sank down on the edge of the table and looked around the bleak room. "Do you remember when we were in here last time?"

Ali nibbled on her bottom lip. "I was thinking about that when I was coming up here. I was just waiting for that Sergeant Lewis to find me, yell at me and push me in here." Ali laughed, a tight, nervous sound. "You know, this place even smells the same way it did back then."

Exactly what she'd thought, and it brought the hint of a smile. "Boy, you've got a memory like an—"

"Don't say it." She patted her tummy under the loose pink material. "I feel big enough as it is without having the word *elephant* brought up."

Alicia felt her throat tighten. "I'll miss seeing that little hoodlum when you have him."

"It could be a her, and you won't miss it. You'll be here. You have to be."

Any suggestion of humor was gone. "I wish I could be." And she meant it. She hated the sense that some bond was about to be torn apart, and for someone who had fought bonds all her life, it surprised her that the idea of breaking this one scared her. "I just can't let you get in the middle of this again. And I can't let the baby get involved. God, I'd die before I'd let anything happen to either one of you, or Lydia, or Jack."

The door opened abruptly, and as if saying his name had conjured him up, Jack Graham hurried into the room. Alicia watched him swing the door shut, then turn to look first at her, then Ali. The jacket of his well-cut gray suit was open, the dark tie loosened. His sandy hair looked as if he'd run his fingers carelessly through it, and his jaw, marred by a jagged scar that cut across his chin, was set in a hard line. Tension bracketed his mouth and narrowed his blue eyes.

Since Ali had met Jack fourteen months ago, they had been inseparable. They'd married after knowing each other only two weeks, and if the baby was a surprise, it was a surprise that both of them welcomed. And Lydia was thrilled, saying that dear Harry should have been around to see their Alison become a mother.

Right now, all Alicia could think of was that Jack knew what was going on. She watched him cross to his wife, put his arm around her and draw her to his side. His hold on her tightened for a minute, but his eyes were on Alicia. "I'm sorry I had to get you here this way, but when I called the house, Lydia said you'd just left for the airport. I needed to see you before you took off. The captain agreed and offered to have one of his men bring you in."

"Jack, this is all about George Terrine, isn't it?"

He looked surprised at her question. "How did you—?"

She hugged her purse tightly. "I knew it was just a matter of time, no matter what you or anyone else said. He's coming after me."

"Alicia—"

"George Terrine is going to kill me, probably have Sharp do it, so I'm leaving. I love you both, but I'm out of here. I'm not going to be a sitting duck, and I'm not going to let the Terrines hurt you both anymore. I can't—" As she started to move toward the door, Jack let go of Ali and blocked Alicia's escape by stepping in front of her. "Jack, please, I have to go."

"No, you don't. You don't have to go anywhere. There is no Sharp. He's gone for good." Jack paused. "George Terrine was found dead in his penthouse apartment in Las Vegas less than an hour ago."

Alicia could feel her jaw drop. "What?"

"He's dead, Alicia."

"Dead?" She seemed incapable of anything more than monosyllabic questions.

"Yes. It looks as if he had a heart attack. Natural causes. One of his employees found him."

Alicia slowly moved back and sank down on the edge of the table. She closed her eyes, her purse clutched to her midsection. "Dead," she whispered, and wondered why there was no coherent reaction beyond stunning numbness. "Are you sure?"

"Absolutely. Tom Storm called fifteen minutes ago to tell me."

"Did Sharp—?"

"No, I told you, Sharp's gone. When he was released for lack of evidence in the son's death, he left. No one's heard from him since."

She opened her eyes. "Terrine just died?"

"It looks that way. I wanted to tell you before you took off for Denver and heard it on the radio or television."

"I..." She shook her head as her feelings began to clarify. There was a certain sense of rightness about George Terrine dying alone. The man had wanted to kill her. He'd sent his men after her. They hadn't known they were really following *Ali,* that she'd had her twin take her place. They just knew that they were to kill Alicia Sullivan so she couldn't go in front of the grand jury with testimony that would assure the indictment of Mick Terrine on first-degree murder charges. He'd had his own son killed.

She moistened her lips and straightened to look at Jack and her sister. "I...I have to leave."

"Alicia, please, you don't have to run away," Ali said softly, her hand on her sister's arm.

She looked into Ali's green eyes, seeing the pain there, the fear that the past was going to repeat itself, that she'd take off and never look back. "I'm not running away, Ali. I have to go to Colorado."

Ali pulled Alicia into a hug that almost took her breath away. "Yes, now you can fly off to Colorado and really start a new life without any bogeyman from your past rearing his ugly head," Ali whispered in her ear before she withdrew.

Bogeyman. That's exactly what Terrine had been. That element of her life that gave her nightmares, that had made her look over her shoulder, that had made her feel as if she would never be able to put her past mistakes behind her. But he was gone. It was all over, and it felt as if a huge weight had been lifted from her soul.

A new life. Alicia felt almost light-headed at the prospect of the past really being over and done. The future was hers for the making. Whatever she did with it was totally up to her now. "It's finally over," she whispered.

"And you can start to make plans with Jon."

Alicia looked at Ali, her mind blank. "What?"

"Jon. Jonathan Welsh, that hunk you met two months ago at the travel agency. The banker. Blond, good-looking, a bit sober, but nice. The man who asked you to Colorado to spend New Year's with his family at their skiing lodge. The man who's asked you to marry him."

Jon. She tried to focus on Jon, the man who could be her whole future. But all she seemed capable of coping with was the next moment, and that meant getting to the airport. She glanced at the clock. "I don't think I can make my flight."

"Don't worry. I got you an escort to the airport," Jack said. "If I have to, I'll pull some strings and have them hold the flight for you." He strode to the door and tossed over his shoulder, "You'll make it. I promise. Have a good flight." Then he was gone, the door clicking shut after him.

"Trust Jack. When he makes a promise, he keeps it," she heard Ali say.

Alicia stared at the door, then turned to Ali. "It's finally over. All my mistakes, my foolishness, and now I have to make the future work."

"You will. You're doing fine, just as long as you don't leave the way you did the last time we were in here." Her mouth tightened with tension. "Don't you ever leave me again. I swear, if you do, I'll—"

"I swear that I won't," Alicia said, then patted Ali's stomach. "I'll be here for you and sweet pea for the rest of my life." She felt the baby kick, a soft flicking that felt like a little hiccup. She smiled, the expression coming so easily that it shocked her. "I think the baby plans to hold me to that."

"I'm going to hold you to it," Ali said solemnly. "I never want to lose you again."

Alicia drew her hand back and made a cross over her heart, then held up her hand palm out. "Cross my heart and hope to—" She stopped her own words, then said, "I promise you, I'll never leave you again."

Chapter 1

Colorado, December 29, 4:00 p.m., MT

"I'll be coming for you in four days. By this time next week, you'll have disappeared off the face of the earth."

Steven Rider sat deep in the leather chair, warmed by the blazing fire in the massive stone fireplace of the cabin in the high Rockies. He'd met the caller on the end of phone line twice. Once when the slender, dark-skinned man had been introduced as "Sampson" and his contact with the FBI. The second time when Sampson had flown Steven by private jet to Colorado and had driven him to this cabin. No first name, no title, no small talk. Just anonymity, all cloak-and-dagger games.

Steven closed his dark eyes. He was tired of the games. Ever since all hell had broken loose a month ago, he'd been living in the middle of a game. Hide at a safe house in Houston; go to the airport in a florist truck; fly out secretly; come up here at night, crouched on the back floor of an innocuous sedan, and stay out of sight in this isolated cabin rented under the name Joe Riley until after New Year's.

Games. All of it. And he'd be glad to see the end of them.

"Promises, promises," Steven muttered as he opened his eyes and shifted lower in the soft leather. He eased his legs out straight, making sure he didn't bump the dog stretched out on the braided rug in front of the raised hearth. His lanky, six-foot-three-inch frame felt cramped. His muscles were tight and uncomfortable, the way his spirit felt confined. He'd be more than ready to leave when he got the word.

"I guess it's no way to be spending the holidays," the voice on the phone line cut into his thoughts, "alone and cut off, but there wasn't any alternative. They came too close to finding you in Houston."

"How did they get so close?"

"Who knows. Just take comfort in the fact that it will be damn near impossible for them to find you where you are now."

"Damn near?" he echoed skeptically.

"There's no guarantees. You knew that when you agreed to do this."

"Yeah, I knew that," he muttered. He'd figured that out years ago. No guarantees in this life.

He stared at the sleeping dog. The animal had appeared at the cabin two days ago, sitting at a distance, watching while Steven carried wood inside. When he'd gone back out for more wood, the dog was still there, just waiting.

He was large and heavy-boned, a cross between a German shepherd and a question mark, with a black coat, butterscotch markings, ears that couldn't decide if they wanted to stand up or flop down and a tail that curled over his back in a plume. The animal's breath had drifted into the cold air, and the dog had slowly come toward Steven, who had been on the porch by the front door.

He still wasn't quite sure why he hadn't gone into the house and shut the door. The animal had looked as if he could take care of himself, as if he hadn't needed anyone. And maybe that was it. Steven had felt a certain kinship with the animal's aloneness. "He's a survivor," Steven could remember thinking just before he'd stepped back and let the dog into the warmth of the cabin.

That had been a couple of days ago, and the animal was still there. When Steven left, he knew the dog would move on to the next person who would take him in, let him sleep in front of a fire and give him food. Take what he needed, then move on. A bit like himself, he supposed.

"Rider? You still there?"

"Yeah," Steven said. "How about Shaw or Sanbourn, or whatever-the-hell name he's going by? Is he still where he's supposed to be?"

"Last time I checked."

"Keep him there."

"That's the plan," Sampson said. "Hope the solitude up there isn't getting to you."

The man had no idea that being alone, for Steven, wasn't on par with loneliness. He was used to being alone. He had been since he'd run away from home when he was sixteen. It didn't matter if he was hitching his way across country or working in construction or doing what he'd done during the past year, being the bodyguard for one of Houston's biggest names in the business world. He'd learned to lean on no one, depend on no one and keep his own counsel.

"I'm fine." He shifted to sit up and saw the dog stir. "And I'll be even better if everything's worked out for the move after I give my testimony."

"That's all set."

"That's all I need to know."

"Good, because that's all I can tell you right now." Sampson hesitated, then asked a personal question, something he'd never done before. "Any regrets?"

"Plenty, but not about doing this."

"No second thoughts about what you're giving up?"

The answer came without hesitation. "None." At thirty-seven years of age, Steven had found out long ago that he had nothing in this life he couldn't give up if he had to. There had never been anyone. No close friends. No family. For a flashing moment, that idea was oddly disturbing.

His relationships with women were fleeting, relegated to shadows of the past, occasionally flitting in and out of his mind. The bottom line was that none of them really mattered for more than the moment. "I guess I could have saved myself all this trouble if I hadn't done my job protecting Shaw so well," he said wryly. "I should have let some of his so-called peers get to him."

"Your employer wasn't exactly well loved," Sampson murmured.

"*Former* employer, and everyone seemed to hate his guts. That's why he had me. The guy's obnoxious and aggressive. Stupid, too. Seems to me if he was working on a new identity that he would have kept a lower profile, but he never did."

"With the plastic surgery and the changes he made, no one even suspected he was Bryce Sanbourn until you stumbled across the truth."

Stumbled was the right word. Steven had come back to work after a few days off when he'd heard things he shouldn't have heard and seen things he shouldn't have seen. And if Bryce Sanbourn, Shaw's original identity, hadn't been a drug trafficker, he probably would have walked away without a word. He would have left, looked for another job and never told anyone that Sanford hadn't died in New York. But Clarence Shaw had been born and, using the cover of a respectable businessman, had kept up his old activities.

Steven wasn't a moralizer or a do-gooder by any stretch of the imagination. He'd cut corners and shaved the truth himself enough times in his life, but drug dealing wasn't something he could turn his back on. His father's use of alcohol, his drug of choice, had devastated everyone the man touched. "He supposedly made a new man out of himself," he said to Sampson.

"I imagine you can relate to that—becoming a new man."

Sampson was serious, but to Steven the words were the first joke he'd heard in a while. They almost made him smile. Almost. He raked his fingers through the straight ebony hair that fell to his shoulders and exhaled harshly. "Yes, I suppose I can."

No one, least of all Sampson, knew that he'd lived through it once already when he ran away from home twenty-one years ago. He'd left behind Stevie Ryder, and Steven Rider had been born. Steven Rider had no history of a father who had beat him, no history of a father who drank himself into a stupor, no history of a mother who just gave up and died early, and no history of being afraid all the time.

Steven Rider made his own fate, and now he was giving up Steven Rider by his own choice. It was simple. But others wouldn't understand that.

"I should get going," Sampson said, "but I wanted you to know that everything's on track."

"Good."

"One more thing."

"What's that?" Steven asked.

"Don't count on being safe anywhere. Shaw's not stupid, and if we can hide you, he can find you. He proved that in Houston. Keep your eyes open. Don't trust anyone, and call the number if there's any trouble. I'll call one more time to give you the final timetable. And take care."

Without waiting for a reply, Sampson hung up.

Steven leaned to his right to put the receiver back in the cradle, then stood. The dog twisted and looked back over his shoulder at Steven. "What's your problem?" Steven asked. The dog lifted one butterscotch-colored eyebrow at him, then slowly got to his feet. "It's not dinnertime yet."

Steven crossed the plank floor and took his leather aviator jacket off one of the pegs driven into the log wall by the heavy wooden door. He slipped it on over his T-shirt and jeans, pushed his feet into the heavy snow boots, and before he could reach for the door-knob, the dog was at his side. He looked down at the animal, meeting the unblinking dark stare, and he shook his head. "Damn, you can read minds, can't you? Well, come outside with me if you want to." He zipped up the front of his jacket. "Or stay inside if you want."

He opened the door and frigid air swept into the cabin. As he flipped up the lamb's-wool collar of his jacket, he looked out at the land around the cabin. He'd cleared a pathway in the calf-deep snow between the front door and detached garage, about twenty feet, then a side path to the wood storage lean-to on the southern side of the cabin. But he hadn't bothered clearing the semicircular drive that went to the road where open gates were attached to stone pillars set in a low stone wall.

He wasn't going anywhere, at least not now.

The dog brushed past Steven, stepped out onto the cleared porch, then turned to look up at Steven ques-tioningly. "All right," he muttered, "so I don't usu-ally go out while it's light. But I need some fresh air." He shook his head and freed his hair from the collar of his jacket. "Damn it all, why am I explaining myself to a mangy dog?"

He pulled the door shut, stepped past the animal, then pushed his hands into the pockets of his jacket. His chin tucked into the fur of his collar, he stepped down off the porch to head for the garage area. His route for exercise was limited to going between the house and garage, or back behind the cabin to the higher land of the foothills at the base of the moun-tains that confined the valley.

Even though he had yet to see anyone drive past, and there wasn't any chance of anyone being close enough to see him, he stayed low. "Not much traffic, and plenty of land as a buffer—over five acres," Sampson had told him when he handed him his ID packet for Joe Riley just before he'd left Steven at the cabin. "The closest neighbor is more than four miles down the road, so there isn't any reason for anyone to even know you're here."

Steven had taken the packet and tossed it into a drawer by the stove in the kitchen. "All right, I'm Joe Riley for now."

"Good. Let's hope you don't have to use it before we get you out of here."

Steven walked slowly along the cleared path and glanced up at the sky. It was bright overhead, but as he looked to the east and off into the distance, he could see dark clouds gathering. The peaks of the towering mountains were already obscured. A storm was coming. He could almost smell it in the cold air.

He'd check on the backup generator in the garage and restock wood for the fireplace from the lean-to, just in case he needed it. As he neared the stone-and-log garage, he looked back at the clouds that rose high and dark into the late afternoon sky.

Uneasiness slid up his spine, but it didn't have anything to do with what he'd face in four days. Or with the fact that Steven Rider would soon cease to exist. Things didn't feel right, and he'd had that feeling often enough in his life to know it was usually accurate.

The dog stopped abruptly, and Steven almost stumbled over him. "Damn it, what's . . . ?" he began, but his voice died out as he watched the animal lift his head. He sniffed the air, then a ridge of fur stood on end along the animal's spine and he howled, an eerie sound that echoed on the cold, clear air.

So, the dog felt it too.

Alicia drove into Gibson, Colorado, just as a billowing bank of dark clouds began to spill over the tops of the encircling mountain range. The sun grew dimmer, and a breeze began to tease the foliage of ancient firs, swirling day-old snow into the frigid air.

Alicia snapped on the headlights of the rental car she'd picked up at the Denver airport and glanced around the village that was backed by a crisscross of ski slopes off to the east. On the cobbled main street, quaint, peak-roofed buildings clustered in the growing shadows, splashes of pure primary colors trimming their eaves and marking their doors.

Slush and snow had been pushed to the sides of the narrow streets, old-fashioned street lamps lined the way, and license plates from various states were visible on the mostly upscale cars. Hand-carved wooden signs swung slowly in the breeze in front of stores displaying designer products in their windows.

Obviously money had found a home in Gibson, an echo of the larger-scaled Aspen, and she wasn't surprised that Jon's family had a winter vacation home nearby. The Welshes had more than enough money to fit right in. She drove slowly, then finally spotted a service station set in between a ski shop and a restaurant that looked like a huge Victorian house.

She pulled off the street and drove in next to the pumps. But before she could get out, an attendant was at the door, a slender teenager wearing a bulky down jacket, stretch ski pants and a broad, expectant smile. She rolled down the window, and the kid said in a quick, cheerful voice, "Welcome to Gibson Village Service Center. Unleaded, super-unleaded or diesel?"

She glanced at the fuel gauge. Half-full. She shook her head. "None, thanks, but I—"

"Check your oil, water, tires? Treat your windows?"

"No, I—"

"Coffee, espresso, hot chocolate, home made cookies?"

"Directions," she said quickly before he could start up again. "I need directions."

"Yes, ma'am." He nodded. "Where to?"

"Harvester Road."

"No problem." He leaned down and rested both hands on the door as he explained. "You go the way you're heading for about six miles and you'll see a sign for Harvester Road. That's a great skiing area. It's more remote than most and the estates are pretty well protected. You won't see too many houses, so watch out for signs that are on the road."

"Thanks," she said.

"Sure you don't want something warm to take with you, compliments of the management?"

The cold air was working its way in through the open window. "Maybe hot chocolate?"

He smiled at her, then jogged toward the office that looked like a Swiss cottage. In just a moment he was back out with a large foam cup and handed it to her through the window.

"Thanks," she murmured, feeling the warmth of the cup as she gripped it.

"Good thing you don't have too far to go, ma'am—there's a big storm coming tonight. Great for skiing, but rotten for driving."

She glanced past him at the almost black clouds that were moving in an angry, tumbling roll across the heavens. "It's going to snow?"

"That's what the weatherman said."

"Then I'd better get going," she said as she put the cup of chocolate in the holder on the dash.

"Take care," she heard the attendant say as she rolled the window up, shutting out the cutting chill of the late afternoon air. She drove back onto the street, headed north, and in just a few minutes, she was on a narrow, two-lane road that headed deeper into a higher level of the valley.

She'd never been in this sort of country before, with towering mountains, winding roads and a cold wind that shook the small car from time to time. Snow had been cleared from the road, and it was piled over three feet high on either side.

She flipped the heater on high, sipped a bit of the rich chocolate and thought how much everything had changed for her. For the best, she told herself, for the best. Even George Terrine's death was for the best. And coming here to meet Jon's family was definitely for the best.

Jon had told her all about his younger brother, older sister, his mother and father and two cousins that would be at the family home for the holidays. Nerves fluttered in her stomach, and that shocked her. "What are you worried about?" she demanded of herself. "You never worry about what people think of you, even people like the Welshes who could buy and sell the state of Colorado.''

Jon never made a big display of his money. Oh, he dressed well, drove a high-end BMW and wore his Princeton pin, but he wasn't condescending. Maybe a bit stuffy now and then, but that could change. She sure had changed. She knew others could.

She rounded a curve in the road, then drove straight for over a mile before she spotted a road sign in the dimness. As her headlights flashed over it, she saw the hand-carved legend—Harvester Road, North. An arrow pointed to the right. She turned north and realized how deserted it was around here. She'd expected expensive homes dotting the area, but as far as she could see into the dimness all around, the land was empty.

Huge firs and deepening shadows surrounded her as it started to snow. Alicia slowed the car, switched on the windshield wipers and watched the soft white flakes drifting from the dark sky. She'd never seen snow falling before; she'd always seen it once it was on the ground. It looked almost magical. She slowed even more, and had a passing idea of feeling the snow on her skin and tasting it on her lips and making snow angels.

But right then the wind shook her car and the snow began to fall harder, the soft flakes now replaced by what looked like white bullets driving down from the skies. She pressed the accelerator and kept going. ''The sooner I get to Jon's, the better,'' she told herself.

Visibility was almost gone, the white snow obliterating anything more than ten feet in front of the car. She could feel the car wandering from side to side, as if an invisible hand were pushing at it. Then she caught a flash ahead. As she saw the arrow warning about a sharp left curve in the road, she stepped on her brakes to slow down.

Without warning, the car went out of control. It began to fishtail violently, then, as if it were floating on air, it glided straight ahead. No matter how she tugged the wheel or screamed or pressed the brake pedal, the car kept going with a mind of its own, sailing into the darkness and the storm.

In that instant, Alicia fully understood the perverted sense of humor Fate possessed. She'd just been freed from the threat of being killed by the Terrines. She'd changed. She'd fixed her life. She was sensible and sane. She was doing things by the book, even thinking about marrying a nice, stable man, and now she was going to die plunging off a cliff on a snowy road in Colorado.

Chapter 2

When they lost their chance to take care of things in Houston, Shaw's people bided their time until they found out that Sampson was in charge of protection for Rider. Then they contacted Jaimie L. in Seattle. He lived under the same name he'd used when he was working with Sampson at the Agency, Lewis Sobba. And until the Agency had released him for being "psychologically unfit for fieldwork," he and Sampson had worked together for three years. He knew Sampson, and he knew how he thought.

When he got the call for the job, Jaimie had named his price. He knew Rider. He'd seen him once at Shaw's house. And he still had contacts that could get a location. All he had to do was wait two hours, put in a call, then let his wife know he'd be gone on "business" for a few days.

When he found out Rider was at station seven under the name of Joe Riley, he skimmed back his thinning brown hair from his pale face and actually smiled. Easy money. The job would be over before Sampson knew he'd been had.

Despite what Alicia had always heard, her life hadn't flashed before her eyes as she'd braced herself to die. She'd closed her eyes and felt a deep regret for all she'd left unsaid and undone, and a terrible sense of sadness that she hadn't been able to keep her promise to Alison. She was leaving her sister again.

But there was no heart-stopping plunge, no horrific crunch of metal tearing and ripping. Just a gliding stop, a wrenching shudder that ran the length of the car, then the motor stopped. The only sounds were of wind, driving snow and the slapping of the wipers on the windshield.

She hadn't died. She was very much alive. She sucked in a breath and felt it fill her tight lungs. The steering wheel was biting into her hands. As she opened her eyes, she could see the blizzard whipping against the car's windshield and the faint, almost watery glow of the headlights ahead.

She forced her hands to let go of the steering wheel and sank back in the seat. The windows to the right were completely blocked by snow, and to the left all she saw was the storm and the night. She couldn't tell if she was on the road, facing forward or backward, but there had been no cliff and no plunge off a mountain.

With a trembling hand, she turned off the headlights and windshield wipers, then turned the key in the ignition. "Come on, come on," she muttered as the starter clicked twice before the motor kicked in. As it idled, she whispered, "All right," then flipped the headlights and windshield wipers back on, slipped the car in gear and pressed the accelerator.

Tires spun, the car lurched, but Alicia felt her heart drop when the car didn't move forward. "It's like mud," she told herself. "Rock it out." She put the transmission in reverse, then into drive, then into reverse again, and although the car lurched back and forth, it didn't go anywhere. When she stopped, it simply sank back into its original position.

Alicia hit the steering wheel with the heel of her hand and muttered an oath she hadn't used for years. "Think, think, think," she hissed. "What are you supposed to do when you get stuck in snow?" If the car was stuck, so was she.

She sank back into the seat and tried to see outside. But there was nothing except darkness and storm, and the dull glow of the headlights showed the snow being driven by the wind. Stories about cars being stuck in blizzards, then being found days later with dead bodies in them, flashed through her mind.

"I am not going to be one of those people," she promised herself. "Not now, not after everything I've gone through to get here. I didn't give up smoking just to become healthy and then have this happen." She glanced at the fuel gauge. A quarter of a tank. She didn't know how that translated into minutes that the car could keep running and keep the heater going for warmth before stalling, but she knew it wouldn't be all night.

She flicked the heater vent so it blew right at her, turned off the windshield wipers that were vainly trying to keep the glass free of snow, and flicked off the headlights. "What are the options? Get out and look for help, or stay in the car and wait for help to find me?" They didn't sound too good, and even though she wasn't that far from Gibson, she might just as well be at the end of the earth.

Wind jarred the car, and snow drove against its exposed side. With a shudder, she tugged her coat more tightly around her. "All right. I'll stay in here for a while. Maybe the storm will stop soon and I can see where I am. Maybe I'll get lucky and someone will come by, like a search team looking for people who got stranded."

She couldn't be the only person driving tonight. Wind howled outside, mingling with the sounds of driving snow, and Alicia reached for the radio and flipped it on. There was static and interference; then she found a station. The strains of "oldies, but goodies" filled the car, and Alicia snuggled into the corner of the car against the door.

After a few minutes, a news flash interrupted the music for a newscaster to warn about a heavy storm that was making its way through the Rockies. "And when the storm's over, it looks like we'll have excellent skiing conditions for the New Year," he assured the listening audience, then music started up again.

"Sure, excellent," she muttered, but in the meantime, she knew the car was being buried by the storm.

She glanced at the fuel gauge again. It was lower, closer to Empty than to the quarter-tank mark. "Another ten minutes, then I'll..." Her voice trailed off. "Do what?" she asked herself. "Go skiing?"

She closed her eyes and was surprised that now was the time her life flashed in front of her. The early years, her parents dying when she and Alison were five, the foster homes, then Lydia and Harry taking them in and giving them a real family.

Then her restlessness, high school, leaving to travel, wandering around, looking for something she never found, then meeting Mick Terrine. *The moment of truth.* Alicia had understood that completely during that time last year. Maybe she'd grown up...finally. She'd met Jon. *Jon.* She tried to focus on his face, but for a horrifying moment, she couldn't get a clear mental picture of him. Then it came, but it was blurred and without definition.

She sat up, rubbing a hand over her face. She couldn't wait here much longer. "No one's coming. Jon won't even know I'm missing until it's too late. Why didn't I let him meet me in Denver, or, at least, meet me in Gibson? He wanted to. He offered to, but no, I had to tell him I'd get there on my own."

She had known Jon was annoyed. He liked things neat and under control. That was partly why she'd quit smoking. He didn't like smoking. He thought people who smoked didn't have control. He'd probably been right. That control had extended to him knowing exactly where she was, when she'd get there, and how she'd get there. But he'd finally agreed to let her do it her way. Having a fight was just another way of losing control for Jon. He definitely wasn't a fighter.

So now Jon would think she was on her way, Alison would think she was at Jon's, and she'd be freezing to death in some rental car. Snow had banked against the front window and the storm wasn't lessening. If anything, it was getting worse. She wished she had a cigarette right now.

She exhaled. "I am *not* going to freeze to death in this car," she muttered to herself, and got on her knees to reach back over the front seat to open the suitcase she'd brought. She flipped it open and rummaged around until she found ski gloves, a wool ski hat with a face mask and a down jacket.

They were all new, bought just for this trip, and she hoped they were warm. The saleslady had said they looked good, that the bronze color of the jacket complemented her hair, but she'd never mentioned warmth. Even the fleece-lined boots she was wearing looked good, but she didn't even know if they were waterproof.

At least they would give her some protection while she waited. She took off her light jacket, put the other one on over her sweater, and after she twisted her hair into a loose knot, she tugged the cap on over it. As she settled back behind the wheel, the car sputtered and the motor stopped. One glance at the gas gauge and she knew her options were growing fewer and fewer. The needle was on Empty.

"All right," she told herself. "I'll walk. Jon's place can't be much farther down the road."

She took her wallet out of her purse, grabbed the car keys and put them in her pocket. With a deep breath she swung the door open. "Here goes nothing," she muttered as the wind pushed the door outward. The air was biting and fierce outside.

Alicia tugged her jacket collar higher, pulled the protective ski mask down over her face, then quickly put on the gloves. As she stepped out into the storm, she steadied herself with one hand against the side of the car, then hit the lock and fought to close the car door.

She stood very still for a minute in snow that was calf-deep while she tried to look around. But when she raised her head, the snow stung her face, even through the protection of the wool. Ducking her chin protectively into the collar of her jacket, she aligned herself with the front of the car and started walking straight ahead, hoping against hope she wouldn't walk off a cliff.

Trying to move in the deep snow was almost like walking in mud. It caught at her legs, made her feet feel as if they weighed a ton, and it felt as if she were walking in slow motion. Worse yet, the color-coordinated clothes were little protection after all. Cold was seeping through the jacket and hat, and snow was working its way down the top of her boots. She bowed her head lower and trudged forward, praying she was going in the right direction.

Her legs ached horribly, and the air she drew into her lungs through the slit in the ski mask was so cold it felt as if she were inhaling fire. She lifted her head just a bit, narrowing her eyes against the driving snow, and she tried to look ahead. The pelletlike snowflakes stung where her face was exposed, and no matter how hard she tried, she couldn't see more than five feet ahead of her. Darkness and storm swallowed up the world.

She curled her hands into fists in her pockets, bunching the material of her gloves with her tingling fingers. She was close—she had to be. The thought was a comfort of sorts until she realized Jon's house could be right next to her and she wouldn't be able to find it.

She trudged forward, her legs stinging with wet cold. Why hadn't she let Jon do it his way? Why had she reverted to type, not wanting to be controlled, not wanting to be pinned down by specifics? Maybe she'd changed, but there were still remnants of the past clinging to her like cobwebs, and just as annoying.

She was beginning to feel exhausted, and she stopped, using her hand to protect her eyes. She couldn't see anything, and she knew that she couldn't go much farther. She turned her back to the wind, trying to catch her breath, and was shocked when she thought she saw a momentary flicker of light off to her left.

But when she looked again, it was gone. "Damn it, you're hallucinating," she whispered, her lips feeling oddly numb.

There was nothing but snow and night. She cupped her tingling hands around her eyes, and she prayed for the light to appear again. Nothing. Did people who died in blizzards hallucinate?

Just then she saw it again, a faint flash in the darkness, but it disappeared again. She lunged forward, staggering for a minute in the snow that was now almost up to her thighs. The light was there again, then gone, and she felt panic choke her. Another step, then another, in the direction of the light. She was between two massive snowdrifts, then she was at a huge tree. She reached out, touched the dark trunk and gave herself a minute to take advantage of what little protection it offered.

"Keep going," she told herself silently, unable to form words any longer. "Keep going." She kept her hand on the trunk as she moved around the tree, lifting her feet as high as she could.

She saw the light, closer than before, and she let go of the tree trunk. Closer, clearer, a beacon through the snow and night. The tree branches must have been blocking it from her before. But it was there now. And it was real, not a hallucination. She waded through the snow, almost falling, but she kept going.

Her face ached, her hands and feet were numb, but the light was like a magnet, drawing her forward. She tried to breathe through her teeth, her chest and throat on fire. She moved awkwardly, almost with swimming motions, pushing at the snow with her hands, flailing to make any progress, terrified that if she took her eyes off the light, it would disappear for good.

Then her foot struck something covered by the snow, and she tumbled forward. She screamed as she plunged to the ground, her hands tunneling through the soft flakes as she landed facefirst in the cold. She twisted to one side, struggling to get up, but ended up on her back with the sky above her.

In that instant everything changed. The cold was gone as the storm drifted off into the distance, and a strange warmth wrapped around her. She turned onto her side, pulled her knees up to her stomach, folded her numb hands under her cheek and closed her eyes. Maybe she'd rest here for a minute, just long enough to get her strength back so she could make it to the light.

The blizzard began to die down about the same time the dog got restless. Steven looked away from the book he was reading in the leather easy chair by the fireplace and watched the animal stir. Lying on the braided rug in front of the hearth, the animal stretched, sighed, then stilled. But before Steven could start reading again, the dog was moving. He got to his feet, slowly crossed to the door, pushed his nose against the spot where the door met the jamb, and began to whine.

After a moment, he turned and pinned Steven with his unblinking gaze. Then the whine turned to a rumbling growl and the fur rose in a ridge along his back.

The irritation Steven felt at being disturbed fled when the dog growled and turned back toward the door, scratching at it with his paw. Steven never took his eyes off the door as he lowered the book to the floor by the chair, then got to his feet. Something was wrong. Someone or something was out there. He could almost feel it, and the familiar adrenaline that imminent danger produced surged through him.

He reached for the phone, but the line was dead. There wasn't even a buzz. He was on his own, just the way he had been most of his life, and without hesitating, he hurried into the kitchen to get his gun. He grabbed the automatic off the top of the refrigerator along with a clip, loaded it, tested it, then went back into the living room.

No one should be anywhere around the cabin. Sampson had assured him no one ever came this way. So that meant one of two things. Either the dog was just nervous because of the storm, or someone hired by Shaw had tracked Steven down.

He headed for the door and ran his free hand over the light switch. As the cabin slipped into darkness, except for the flickering glow of the fire in the hearth, Steven reached for his jacket and boots and put them on. He wasn't going to sit in here like some sitting duck and wait to be taken out.

There was no other way out of the cabin but the front door, so that was the way he had to go. He gripped the door knob and slowly inched the barrier back until he could see outside through an inch-wide gap.

The ferocity of the storm had all but slipped away, and it had left a sprinkling of flakes in the air and a sky with a nearly full moon coming out from behind a low bank of clouds. The silvery shimmer touched the land around the cabin, bathing it in stark whites and blacks, all colors gone. A breeze drifted through the frigid air, and the huge firs that rimmed the front of the property were hulking shadows, blanketed under the newly fallen snow.

He watched, barely breathing, waiting for a glimpse of movement outside, but nothing stirred that wasn't touched by the breeze. Gripping the gun, he eased the door back just enough to slip outside into the shadows of the porch overhang. Before he could close the door, the dog pushed past him and stopped by his side, silent and still, as if he were scanning the land just the way Steven was doing.

Then abruptly the animal moved. He leapt off the porch into chest-deep snow. Steven stayed in the shadows, watching the animal make his way toward the road. He slowly lowered the gun to his side, narrowing his eyes to try and make out details, but in the moonlight, everything seemed to run from stark light into deep shadows.

If someone from Shaw had found him, Steven was out of here. No more talking. No more trusting men like Sampson. He was on his own, and he'd disappear by himself. Sampson had told him this house was about the safest place to be. But if the man was wrong, it was Steven's life that was on the line. And he wanted control of that life. He didn't want—

His thoughts were cut off when he saw the dog stop, lower his head and start to bark. The sound was deep and cutting, echoing all around. And it didn't stop. Steven moved to the edge of the porch, his free hand reaching out to touch the log wall of the cabin. He could see the dark shape of the dog against the silvered white of the newly fallen snow. Then he gradually became aware of a blur of darkness that looked partially hidden at his feet.

Trying not to expose himself, Steven stayed in the shadows and moved to his left, silently stepping off the edge of the porch into the snowdrift by the wall. He eased along the wall to the corner, then he broke free and moved as quickly as he could to the protection of the garage.

Trees almost touched the far side of the garage and Steven moved to them. When the dog kept barking, Steven stepped away from the garage and into the trees. The sound in the frigid air gave him the creeps, and he found himself trying to hurry, but the snow seemed to pull at his feet, frustrating any attempt at speed.

When he got within ten feet of the road, he shifted the gun, gripping it with both hands, and curled his finger around the trigger. Before he could step clear of the trees, the dog stopped barking and the silence that fell was a shock.

Steven scanned the night, saw nothing beyond the animal, then braced himself, lifted the gun and aimed it ahead of him with both hands. Then he stepped clear of the trees and slowly neared the dog. He darted a look at the dark shape in front of the animal, then scanned from side to side. He couldn't see anything.

Cautiously, he moved even closer and lowered the gun, but he didn't alter his grip. Had the dog found a small animal? A rabbit?

The dog looked up at Steven, then moved back a half pace to let Steven get closer. Steven took another step and knew how wrong he'd been. It wasn't an animal in the snow. He dropped to his haunches as he pushed the gun into his jacket pocket and stared at a person partially covered by snow. He could make out little beyond the fact that the person wasn't moving, had curled into a ball on his side, a full ski mask was in place, and a bulky jacket glistened with dampness.

He reached out and felt the wool of the mask, cold and damp. He moved his hand to the bottom of the mask and into the collar of a heavy down jacket. His fingers felt skin that held a bare trace of body heat. Then he pressed his fingertips to the side of the person's throat. A weak and thready pulse beat against his fingers.

Damn it all, he wasn't in a position to do anything for another person. He could barely keep himself safe. *Safe.* That word brought a thought that shook him. This could be one of Shaw's people, someone who had miscalculated and got stranded before they could get to him. He drew his hand back. He could walk away and pretend that he never saw this. Uncomplicated and safe.

Then he faced a basic fact. He was many things. He was a loner, self-absorbed, and a survivor. But he wasn't a killer. And he didn't have any idea who this person was, anyway. A neighbor? A lost traveler? A hired killer? When the dog nudged at the person in the snow and whined, Steven knew he didn't have a choice.

With a low, vibrating oath that was meant more to make him feel better than to make a difference, he reached out and caught the person's arm. He gripped the heavy coat, tugged on it, and the person rolled toward him, his head lolling to one side. The ski mask seemed almost obscene with its garish knit smile despite the fact that the person wearing it could be dying.

Steven pushed at the snow, thankful that, although the person seemed tall, he wasn't overly big. He worked one hand under the legs and the other under the back. Then, gripping as tightly as he could, he levered himself to his feet. The weight in his arms was bulky and awkward, but remarkably light. He shifted his burden to get a better hold, then started for the house.

His boots sank in the soft snow, making walking almost impossible. In the glow of the moon, he saw the house, a dark shadow through the scattering of snowflakes still falling. For a moment he almost laughed aloud. He could be carrying his own murderer into the house. The irony of the thought only underscored how capricious Fate could be.

The dog bounded ahead of Steven, leaping high to clear the snow, moving with an ease that was enviable. By the time Steven got to the porch, he was breathing hard, and the burden in his arms felt like a ten-ton weight. The dog stopped at the door as Steven took the steps in one long stride. He fumbled for the doorknob, managed to turn it, and when it clicked, he kicked at the barrier and it opened. It hit the inside wall with a cracking thud.

Steven entered the blanketing warmth and flickering shadows, then crossed to the bedroom and eased the person down in the mussed linen of the four-poster bed. Quickly, he stripped off his jacket and tossed it behind him to the floor, then reached to snap on a side light. He stepped out of his boots as he stared down at the figure on the bed.

The person hadn't moved. The limbs were at awkward angles, and the head was turned away from him, lying with the chin tucked into the shoulder. He pushed his boots out of the way, then leaned over the bed and tugged at the ski mask.

As the damp wool slid up, it exposed a face—a woman's face—with a finely drawn chin, full lips that were tinged with a disconcerting blueness, high cheekbones touched with the telltale dead white of frostbite, and closed eyes with incredibly long lashes starkly dark against pale skin. A cascade of wildly curling hair the color of burnished copper spilled free on the white linen. Not the image of a hired gun, for damn sure, he thought as he tossed the hat behind him.

At any other time, he knew he'd be taken by the beauty of the stranger, but right now all he felt was fear. *She* wasn't moving. Her color was horrible, and he knew she was going to die unless he could do something for her and do it fast. Get her warm. Get her color back. And get her to move and open her eyes.

He worked quickly, stripping off her jacket and boots and discarding the cold, wet clothes behind him. She felt like a rag doll, falling back onto the bed, her head lolling to one side. A bulky white sweater and corduroy slacks felt cold to the touch, and the pant legs were dark with moisture. They had to go.

He remembered something from the past, something he'd learned, but he had no idea where he'd learned it or why he remembered it. To get the most body heat possible, a person had be as naked as possible. In the past, he would have laughed at the idea, the perfect way to get a woman out of her clothes and into his bed, but this wasn't a joke. And if he was going to help her, he had to give her the one thing he had that could save her life.

Body heat.

Chapter 3

Steven reached out and touched her hand, shocked at the lack of warmth. Then he steeled himself and stripped off her sweater and corduroy slacks. He tried to ignore the white lacy bra, matching panties, full hips and shapely legs that looked as if they could go on forever. He turned from the sight, tossed her clothes on the pile by the bed, then crossed to the fireplace. He laid more logs on it, prodded life from the glowing embers under the grate, then went back to the bed.

She was just as he'd left her, on her back, her hair spread on the pillows, her hands at her sides. He could see her breathing, a faint feathery motion that looked too insubstantial to support life. He stripped out of his own clothes, down to his shorts, then climbed onto the bed, slid down beside her and tugged the down comforter up over both of them.

He shifted lower, pulled her against him, her back to his chest, her legs arched to fit the angle of his, then he circled her waist with his arm to keep her close. Her curls brushed his face, and she felt so cold against his skin that he could feel the chill seeping into him.

He rubbed her arm with his hand, then her side and her hip, the friction of skin on skin warming his hand, but her skin seemed to refuse to accept any of the heat. He moved closer, putting his leg over her thigh, and his hand slid over her arm, then her side, down to her hip. He felt the curve, the smoothness of her skin, and for a fleeting moment, Steven knew how potent this woman's presence would have been in any man's bed.

The idea rocked him. She was clinging to life, and he was thinking about another scenario altogether. "You've been alone far too long," he whispered through clenched teeth. "Way too long."

He shifted, tugged her over onto her back, then pulled her to him, face to face. For a moment he caught a glimpse of her, the low light etching her face with shadows. But he could still see the horrific paleness. Her lips were softly parted, and he could hear her breathing, a faint rasp behind the exhalation. It shook him to the core to think she could slip away, that she was holding to life by a thin thread and it was all up to him to make sure that thread didn't snap.

He drew her to him, her head heavy on his shoulder, and he rested his chin on her curls. He felt every faint breath she took, her breasts against his chest, her hips against his. And as the minutes ticked by, he could feel heat in him and around him, except where she touched him. He rubbed his hand on her back, harder and harder, frustration welling up in him when she didn't respond.

"What we need is more body heat," he whispered under his breath.

He'd barely uttered the words before the dog jumped onto the bed, landing squarely on the far side of the woman. Steven had forgotten about the animal until now. The dog glanced at him, then, with a throaty sigh, lay down along the woman's back, his muzzle on the pillow by the brilliant curls.

Body heat was body heat. He skimmed his hand over the silky coolness of her arm and held more tightly to her with his other arm. "Come on, damn it, live," he whispered. "Live."

Before his words had died out, he felt her stir. Her breasts moved in a faint, fluttery movement against his chest. She took a breath, a shuddering intake of air, and he didn't move, his hand lying still on her shoulder. Then she exhaled softly, the sound a light sigh, and her hand, which had been pinned between them, opened. Slender fingers spread on his chest. Just as Steven was about to move back to look at her, her arm went around his waist and she snuggled into his side.

Steven closed his eyes tightly and concentrated on the fact that she was going to live. He swallowed hard as her hand moved on his skin, coming to rest over his heart, and tension grew in him. The way her body curved into his, fitting neatly in all the right places, he had the heady thought that it felt as if she had been made just to fit right where she was now.

He shifted and her hair brushed his face, whisper-soft and as seductive as the touch of a rose petal. "A damn poet," Steven muttered.

Rational thought cut through the fantasy. He didn't have a clue about this woman he'd rescued. Beautiful and sexy was one thing. Making him want to lie with her forever was another. But the possibility of her being sent by Shaw was the most important thing. He needed to evaluate the situation, and he couldn't do that with her lying in his arms, as trusting as a small child.

"Yeah, a small child," he ground out as he eased his arm out from under her head. Body heat was all he could afford to share with her. Even though he could feel the way his body was involuntarily responding to the silky softness in his arms, he knew if she moved one more time and he felt her breasts against his chest, he'd explode.

He cautiously moved away from her, blocking out the feeling of his skin where she'd touched him. She shifted, then turned away from him and settled into the pillow with a soft sigh, moving closer to the sleeping dog by her side.

Steven got out of bed, tugging the comforter over her as much to hide the sight of her from him as to keep her warm. He reached for his jacket, took the gun out of the pocket and pushed it between the mattress and the box spring. Then he crouched over the woman's clothes on the floor near the bed and went through them. He found a wallet in the pocket of the jacket, along with a set of car keys marked with the tag of a rental company. That pretty much did away with the idea that she was a neighbor who got lost.

He put the keys back, then opened the wallet. There was a California driver's license made out to one Alicia Sullivan. Age: 28. Height: 5'10". Weight: 115

pounds. Hair: red. Eyes: green. He looked at the picture, the bright curls, the classic features and the smile that tugged at the corners of her full lips. That was the woman in the bed. And the ID looked legitimate enough, but a person working a hit for Shaw wouldn't be an amateur.

He went through the rest of her wallet, took note of the money, almost three hundred dollars, an ATM card for a well-known bank, a few check-cashing cards all in the name of Alicia Sullivan. She only carried two pictures. One of an elderly woman with short gray hair, a round, pleasant face and kind eyes behind thick glasses. The other one was of Alicia with a sandy-haired man who looked uncomfortable sitting for the camera. But there was no mistaking the protective way he held his arm around Alicia's shoulder or the familiar way he touched her cheek against his.

Steven hadn't thought a woman like this would be free, but it was vaguely unsettling to see the way she smiled into the camera. She looked totally happy, as if she'd found the pot of gold at the end of the rainbow or the happily-ever-after ending to a fairy tale. He didn't believe in either. Illusions, that's all they were, and she'd find out soon enough on her own. He pushed the wallet back in the pocket of the jacket and went through the rest of her clothes, but he didn't find anything.

He dropped the clothes back on the floor, then stood by the bed just watching the woman. Her skin was a more normal color now, and her lips had a pale pinkness to them that was welcome after the tinge of blue earlier. He raked his fingers through his long, dark hair, flicking it back from his shoulders as his gaze moved to her left hand, which lay on the linen at her side. No ring. Not even a hint there'd been one there.

"Alicia Sullivan," he said, letting the name touch his tongue. "Alicia." Soft and pretty. The name of a beautiful woman, a woman who could be someone's wife, someone's lover, or... a killer. Nothing surprised Steven anymore, and sending a stunning woman for the hit would sure as hell be a terrific cover. A woman to distract him. She could certainly do that to a man. And he was just a man.

She stirred and whimpered softly. A frown tugged a fine line between her closed eyes, her bottom lip trembled and her whole body began to shiver. The dog stirred, lifting his head to look up at Steven, as if to say, "Well, do something." And Steven did. He moved instinctively, getting back under the blanket with her and pulling her to him. He stroked her hair back from her face, then made slow circles with the palm of his hand against her back.

The trembling started to subside, then, without warning, she slid her hand around his waist and held on to him tightly as her cheek pressed to his chest. The action tugged at Steven, making his heart lurch, and his hand stilled on her.

He wasn't at all sure he should be in this bed with this woman. Every instinct in him was reacting to her closeness again. Damn it, he had always been the one to pick and choose the women he'd spent time with, and especially the women he'd held close to him in bed. He was the one who'd limited a relationship, who'd never stayed the night. He was the one who'd left before there were any demands made of him that he didn't want to meet.

Now here he was with a woman who not only was in his bed, but she was depending on him for everything, including her life. He stared up at the shadowy ceiling, bracing himself when she laid her leg heavily over his thighs in an action of total trust. He bit his lip and closed his eyes.

As the minutes ticked by, Steven held Alicia, listened to her soft sighs in sleep, felt the way her heart fluttered against his ribs, and the effort to stay awake and keep the contact totally platonic was exhausting him. When he could stay awake no longer, he gave in to sleep. If he slept, at least he wouldn't be feeling every curve and softness of the woman in his arms.

He twisted until he could push his free hand between the mattress and box springs and feel the cold metal of the gun. Later he'd find out if he needed the gun or not, but for now, he needed to rest. He breathed deeply and evenly, settled back into the bed. In that moment between waking and sleeping, the irony of his situation struck him again. He'd saved the life of someone who may have been sent to kill him. Then he let go and fell into forgetfulness.

Alicia floated in comfort and warmth. The storm had been a nightmare. The cold wind and snow had all been an illusion, part of a hallucination. This was reality. Being held, being comforted and feeling as if the world was finally right.

She moved closer to the heat with a sigh, then realized that the good feelings had a definite source. As sleep began to slip away, she felt arms and legs and skin. The arms were around her, the legs tangled with hers, and skin was against hers along the length of her body. Skin. Her throat tightened. There was a lot of skin. She could feel hers against it. Skin against skin. His skin against hers. His?

Oh, God. She could barely breathe. She was almost completely naked in some man's bed and she had no idea how it all had happened. Naked. No, she could feel that she had on her panties and bra. But she couldn't be sure if he had on anything. Sleep was gone, and Alicia knew that whatever the dream had been, the reality was that she was in bed with a man. He was at least as tall as she was. Her head was on his shoulder, her hand spread on his stomach, and his legs were a match for hers.

She took a tight breath and caught the scent of soap, heat and maleness all mingled on skin that felt warm and sleek under her hand. She'd been trudging through the snow and storm. She'd been cold, then so tired. Then warm and numb. Now she was here. Her cheek was against his chest, and she could feel the solid, strong beat of his heart.

Damn it, she'd done dumb things in her life, things that weren't thought out very well. Mick Terrine was enough evidence of that. But even with the likes of Mick, there hadn't been any 'lost' nights, or mornings of waking to find herself in bed with a man...any man.

Not even Jon. Jon. That was who this was. Jon. She could deal with that. Someway she'd made her way to Jon's house or he'd found her. This was gratitude. Maybe reaction. A part of her began to relax. Even though she and Jon had talked about sex, and he'd agreed to be patient until she felt right about it, this wasn't all bad. Maybe it had been for the best. Maybe it would help her make up her mind.

But as she opened her eyes, she knew how wrong she was. All she could see was an expanse of bare chest, and her hand lying open on it. But it wasn't Jon's chest. Instead of the soft mat of hair and lightly tanned skin, there was deeply tanned skin. Her fingers were spread on the suggestion of dark hair that formed a T that ran down to disappear under a royal blue comforter. No, this wasn't Jon at all.

She barely took time to realize she was almost relieved he wasn't Jon, before the impact of not knowing the man hit her hard. A strange man. A strange bed. She swallowed hard. *"Just look at him. See who he is, then get the hell out of here,"* she told herself. She braced herself, then slowly shifted back to look up.

She met the gaze of eyes that almost matched the color of the comforter. The stare was penetrating, even partially shadowed by thick dark lashes, and it made her breathing stop. One thing was very certain. She'd never seen this man before in her life.

Alicia made herself keep eye contact, hoping against hope that the man would say or do something so she had a clue as to what was going on. But he kept silent. His eyes were intent, and she had the most awful feeling he was waiting for something. She just wished she knew what.

Slowly she eased back, until she was on one elbow, and the man let his arm slip from around her shoulder to fall to the pillow. Afraid to move anymore, she found herself taking in more and more about the stranger. Beyond the deep blue eyes that had a hint of an exotic slant at the corners, there were high cheekbones, a strong jaw and dark brows. Straight ebony hair fell from a center part, and she thought it probably was at least shoulder-length when the man wasn't lying down.

With his coloring, he looked as if he could be of Indian heritage, or maybe he had a Latin background. Whatever it was, he was a man who was making her more and more uncomfortable. There were no answers coming, and Alicia wondered if he had just as many questions as she did. His blue eyes were direct and assessing, seldom blinking, and they gave away nothing.

Surely if she'd been intimate with him, she'd have some sense of connection, some remnant of memory. But there was nothing. And Alicia was almost certain if something had happened between her and this man, there was no way she could have blanked it out. She could feel his heat under her hand, running along her body. Yes, she would have remembered.

She moved back, awkwardly getting to her knees, and as cool air brushed her skin, she reached for the nearest pillow and pulled it against her for protection. Then she wrapped her arms tightly around the pillow and sat very still. The man didn't move, either. He just watched her in that same intense, yet unreadable way.

It was obviously up to her to make the first move. "What...?" She licked her dry lips and tried again. "Who are you?"

He finally moved. Without saying a thing, he threw back the comforter and got out of bed. For a moment, Alicia was sure that he was naked, but as he stood, she was terribly relieved that he wasn't. But that relief was short-lived when she saw he was wearing a pair of undershorts. The white cotton emphasized his deeply tanned back and muscular legs. Then, as he turned to reach for a pair of jeans that had been discarded on the floor by the bed, Alicia saw his broad chest and muscular abdomen. That's where she'd lain, her hand on the sleek skin dusted with dark hair, her cheek against his heart.

She dragged her eyes away to stare down at the pillow being crushed against her chest. Her disorientation deepened, and she could feel her heart thumping in an irregular rhythm against her ribs.

He answered her question with his own question. "How are you feeling?" His voice was deep and low, the sound touched with shadows, the way the man seemed to be.

She kept staring at the pillow, at her hands that seemed unnaturally red. It was only then that she realized her hands were tingling and her feet ached. She'd been so distracted by this man, by being in his bed, that she hadn't even noticed that before. But now the tingling felt almost painful. She kept her arms around the pillow, but flexed her fingers as she looked up at the blue-eyed man. "All right, I think."

He raked his hands through straight black hair that fell just past his shoulders, combing it back from his face. He frowned at the way she was moving her hands. "Are they painful?"

"Sort of throbbing and tingling."

"Frostbite can do that."

"Frostbite?" The snow...and that feeling of warmth she could remember just before everything went black. She spread one hand palm down and studied it, unnerved at its unsteadiness. "I've got frostbite?" She flexed her hand again, then looked up at him.

He zipped the fly of his jeans, leaving the button undone, and reached out to touch her hand. His heat almost burned Alicia, and she forced herself to not pull her hand back from the contact. He caught the tips of her fingers with his and turned her hand over, palm up. "Your color looks better," he said, then let her go.

She didn't want to ask, "Better than what?" She re-gripped the pillow, and wasn't prepared when the man suddenly touched her cheek, his fingers a light, feathery caress of heat against her skin. Then he cupped her chin in his fingers and tipped her face up toward him. A large man, but gentle, she thought as she fought the urge to close her eyes and shut out this madness. Instead she watched his dark eyes skim over her face.

Then he met her gaze. The impact of the connection only increased her erratic heartbeat and she held her breath, waiting for... She didn't know what she was waiting for, and that only confused her more. As quickly as the connection had been made, it was gone, and the man stood back, straightening to his full height—two or three inches over six feet. He hooked his thumbs in the belt loops of his jeans and spoke in a dispassionate voice, as if he were reading a grocery list.

"You don't look any the worse for wear. Your color's good. No sign of permanent damage. All in all, I'd say you were pretty lucky to get off this easily."

Her tongue darted out to touch her cold lips. *Lucky* was a matter of opinion. *Lucky* would become a fact if she knew what was going on and how she had got into his bed. "How did I get here?" she finally managed.

"In my bed?" he asked.

She could feel the heat in her face, but made herself keep eye contact. "In this place. The last thing I remember is being in the snow, and walking, then lying down and..." She exhaled. "I'm in the dark. I don't have a clue about what happened." She wasn't about to ask how she got undressed. It was obvious there wasn't anyone around who could have done it but this exotic-looking man who watched her so intently.

"I found you in the snow about a hundred yards from the cabin." He motioned to his right with a nod of his head, and his dark hair stirred around his shoulders. "At least, he found you. I followed him. He's no Saint Bernard, but he knew you were out there and went right to you."

She looked around and saw a dog sitting motionless by the fireplace in a living room that was seperated from the sleeping area by a half wall. The dog, which looked as if he might be part German shepherd, watched her, his eyes unblinking, studying her just the way his master had been moments ago.

He'd found her in the snow, and she'd almost frozen to death. "I... I guess I need to thank him, then."

"I don't think thanks will impress him," the man said. "All he worries about is being warm and getting fed."

"What's his name?" she asked as she looked back to the man by the bed.

He shrugged his broad shoulders. "No idea. He's just been hanging out here for a few days until he decides to move on to someone else."

"He's not yours?"

"Hell, no. I don't know where's he's from or where he's going. I didn't figure there was any point in naming him."

"Sad," she murmured, hating the idea of the animal being so temporary that the man hadn't even thought to give him a name. It brought a flash of the past to her, the pain of being "that girl," or "the foster kid." The one who wouldn't be around long enough to bother getting to know.

"How is it sad?" the man asked.

She watched the animal slowly settle in front of the fireplace, then rest his muzzle on his front feet. "He deserves a name, even if it's only for a while," she said, closing her eyes before looking back at the man.

He lifted one dark eyebrow at her. "Why? What difference does it make if he's called Rover or Dog?"

"A name's something special. It's the one thing you have that's all yours."

"You are who you are. A name doesn't make a hell of a lot of difference one way or the other," he countered.

His statement stopped her. Deep inside, she was who she was, even when she and Alison had traded places to fool people. She was always Alicia, and never Alison, not the core of her, or maybe it was her soul. She nibbled on her bottom lip. "And who are you?"

He hesitated, and a glimmer of something flitted across the blueness of his eyes. For a moment she could have sworn it was a touch of uncertainty, but it was gone too quickly for her to fully understand it. "You can call me Buck. How about you? Who did I find in the snow?"

"Alicia Sullivan."

"And what was Alicia Sullivan doing walking in a blizzard?"

"I wasn't walking originally. I was driving, then the storm started and the next thing I knew, my car just went out of control. It landed in a snowbank of some sort and it's stuck. I couldn't get it to move, then the gas ran out. I couldn't just sit there and freeze to death, so I thought I'd walk to get help." She grimaced. "I had no idea how overwhelming a storm could be. I'm not used to snow."

"Where are you from?"

"Los Angeles." She looked away from Buck and glanced around the cabin. The living area seemed to run the full length of the front of the house. The bedroom was at the back, beyond the half wall. And she could see through a door to her right, and into what looked like a kitchen. Curtains were pulled to cover windows on both sides of the fieldstone fireplace, on the far side of the living room, and back by the bed.

The furnishings were sparse but adequate, giving the cabin the feel of a hunting lodge. A deep green leather couch and two green plaid chairs formed a semicircle in front of the hearth. A desk stacked with books stood under one window, a knotty-pine chest was under the other window. In the bedroom, there was just the bed, two nightstands and a highboy done in dark wood.

Buck said something to her, and as she looked back at him, a real truth hit her and hit her hard. She glanced up at the tall, dark-haired man who studied her intently. She was well and truly alone with this man. He'd found her, brought her here, and she owed him her life, but she had no idea who Buck was. None at all. "Did you say something?" she asked.

"Where were you going when the storm hit?"

Even though he had a leanness to him, there were well-defined muscles in the arms he crossed on his broad chest. A tattoo that looked like an oval with a cross inside it was just below his biceps on his right arm.

As she looked back at his face and met his dark gaze, she could barely control a flinch. He'd saved her life, but there was something about him, something that made Alicia uneasy. His eyes narrowed on her, and she knew what that "something" was. The man had a dangerous edge to him. And it shook her when she realized she'd seen the same quality in Mick Terrine. But what was in Mick had been a mere shadow of what was in this man.

Dangerous or not, she wasn't about to admit to him that no one was looking for her. She needed something that would give her protection as long as she was here alone with Buck. And she knew what that would be. "I was going to meet my fiancé, Jon Welsh." The lie almost stuck in her throat, but once it was out, she embellished it, giving the statement as much weight as she could. "He's expecting me, and he'll be out looking for me."

"I doubt that," Buck said. "No one's out in a night like this. I'm sure he'll think you're smart enough to seek shelter and stay put until the blizzard lets up."

"Maybe. But he's pretty determined and protective. Maybe you know his family? They live near here... Jonathan and Cleo Welsh?"

She didn't wait for any response, but kept going in a rush. "The Welshes are the founders of the Unified Bank. My fiancé's grandfather, Jonathan Welsh I, started the bank eighty years ago. Then they expanded, and Jon's father, Jonathan Welsh II, took over as president and—"

"And soon your fiancé, Jonathan Welsh III, will be the successor to the Welsh throne?"

His sarcasm stopped her dead. This whole conversation was ridiculous. There was no reason for lies. All she had to do was get her clothes and get out of here. She didn't need to sit here in her bra and pants, on her knees in this man's bed, clutching a pillow while she tried to erect some sort of protective wall by telling him Jon's lineage. If someone had tried to impress her this way, she would have been more than sarcastic.

Maybe she had tried so hard to change that she'd become a shallow, class-conscious yuppie. The thought gagged her. "He...he'll take over sooner or later," she muttered.

"Where's their house?"

She licked her lips. "Near here."

"Where?" he persisted.

"Harvester Road, down this way."

"I don't think so," Buck said.

"Why?"

"This is Harvester Road North, and your fiancé isn't anywhere around. Trust me. I'd know if he was."

Alicia almost uttered a horrible profanity, but bit her lip hard to keep it in. No one had told her there was more than one Harvester Road. She could have kicked herself for doing this. It would have been so simple to be rational and give in to Jon, to have taken his offer. "Damn it all," she muttered under her breath. "You're a pig-headed jerk."

"What?"

She shook her head. "Nothing. I'm just..." She shrugged. "I'm sorry this all happened. If I can use your phone, I can call Jon. I know he'll want to thank you for all you've done. He can come and—"

"Don't you understand? No one can go anywhere until this storm lets up."

"At least I can call him and let him know I'm safe, that I'm here."

"You can't do that, either. The phones are out. The storm took them out before I found you."

Alicia bit her lip and tried to think. "You have a car, don't you?"

"Sure. A four-by-four."

"Perfect. That'll make it through to Jon's."

"It won't make it out of the garage until the roads are cleared."

The world began to narrow, and it was harder and harder for her to draw air into her lungs. She couldn't be stuck here with this man, not like this. "How soon will the plows be able to clear the roads?"

"Your guess is as good as mine."

"Are you sure you couldn't get out of here?"

"Look, you'd better accept the fact that we're totally cut off, and Jonathan Welsh III is just going to have to be patient until nature runs its course."

Chapter 4

Alicia stared up at Buck. "Until nature runs its course?"

"Looks that way from where I'm standing."

She had no idea what it looked like from where she was sitting and she wasn't about to get up without being dressed. "I . . . I need my clothes."

Abruptly, he bent, and as he straightened with her sweater and slacks in his hands, he winced. "Sorry. They're still damp. I'll lay them out on the hearth to dry."

With that, he went into the living area and crossed to the fireplace. He stepped over the sleeping dog, shook out her clothes, then laid them out on the stone hearth. Alicia watched him, but she found herself staring at his back, the way his muscles rippled with each movement. And his hair. She'd never liked long hair, but somehow she knew long hair suited him. She never let the pillow slip as she forced herself to realign her thoughts. If she was stuck here with him for a while, she didn't want to be thinking foolish thoughts. They had always gotten her into trouble, and she was in enough trouble as it was.

Steven worked quickly, laying out the sweater and corduroy pants. He needed distance between himself and Alicia so he could think clearly, something that was getting harder and harder for him the longer he looked into those clear green eyes. And clothes were a top priority, just about as important as finding out if what she'd been telling him was the truth.

He hadn't heard the name Welsh before. Sampson hadn't mentioned it in the briefing. And anyone in their right mind never would have been driving in this weather. He wished he could get Shaw out of his mind, but that wasn't happening. Send a beautiful woman to kill him. Who'd think of a hired gun looking like that?

He stood and, without looking at Alicia, went back up into the bedroom and crossed to the highboy. He opened the top drawer and took out one of his shirts. If she was sent to take him out, had she set up the scene outside? That didn't seem possible. He knew she'd almost died. That hadn't been planned. And she didn't have a weapon with her. Her ID looked legit.

He stared at the blue cotton of the shirt in his hand. Was she a plant, someone to find out how he was going to testify to before they took him out? God, his head was beginning to throb. Truth was such a scarce commodity in the circles Steven had moved in for so long that he wondered if he'd know it if it walked up and hit him.

He turned with the shirt, and the sight of Alicia was jarring, even though he thought he'd been prepared for it. Her hair tumbled around her pale face, her huge green eyes were watching him, and she still had the pillow clutched to her chest. Who in the hell was Alicia Sullivan? He crossed to the bed and held out the shirt. "You can use this until your clothes dry."

As she took the shirt, her fingers brushed his hand and he literally felt a shock go through him. He drew back quickly. The phones would probably be out for a while, and he could hear the wind starting up again. Alicia wouldn't be able to get out of here or contact anyone for at least twenty-four hours. He hoped that would be enough time to get to the bottom of the situation. And as soon as the phones were fixed, he could contact Sampson. Let the man earn his keep.

He raked his hair back from his face and looked down at Alicia. "I need to get some wood for the fireplace," he lied. There was more than enough wood stored in a side cupboard built into the wall by the hearth.

What he needed was to get of here and see what she'd do when she thought she was alone. He glanced at the slight parting in the curtain by the fireplace, then motioned to the bathroom behind the closed door on the far side of the bed. "The bathroom's in there. There should be hot water, and there are plenty of towels. I'll be back in a few minutes."

Her driver's license had said "green" for the eye color, but it hadn't warned him that they were a pure green and stunningly enhanced by long, dark lashes. Or that one glance from them could scramble his mind. He backed up and reached for the shirt he'd worn earlier.

Quickly, he put it on and kept talking to fill the silence. "I'll make sure we have enough wood to keep the fire going until this storm's gone. As soon as it's clear enough, I'll take care of your car and make sure you get to your fiancé's house."

"I appreciate all you're doing," she said, her voice a combination of velvet and honey. It did strange things to his nerves, and he wondered what would have happened if he hadn't gotten out of the bed when he did.

"I couldn't let you die out there," he murmured as he pushed his feet into his boots with more force than necessary. He wouldn't even think about that moment when he considered leaving her in the snow to die.

Without looking at Alicia, he crossed to get his jacket. As he slipped on the leather-and-fleece protection, she spoke to him.

"Buck?"

When she'd asked him his name, he'd gone blank for a moment. He couldn't remember the cover name Sampson had given him, and admitting he was Steven Rider had been out of the question, so he'd found himself giving her the name of a man he'd met long ago somewhere near New Orleans. He'd been about twenty and had been hitchhiking through the South when he'd been picked up by a man in a long white Cadillac. The man had been huge, with silver hair, and had smoked a thick cigar. And he'd given Steven a ride almost all the way to Florida.

Buck McQueen. Steven still remembered the name and the man's story. It had paralleled Steven's in some ways—leaving home early, being on his own, doing what he wanted, and finally making his fortune. "Did it in straws," McQueen had said around the cigar as he drove down the road through Bayou country. "Can you believe that? Damned plastic straws." He'd grinned at Steven through the haze of cigar smoke. "Just goes to show you, never underestimate the obvious. You could find your fortune there."

Steven had laughed and had forgotten all about it until now. And now this woman was calling him Buck. He deliberately took his time doing up his jacket before he turned to face Alicia. He sensed the dog getting up to come and stand by him, but all he saw was the woman in the bed, still on her knees, his shirt in her hand. There was something about her that seemed to have the effect of a lightning strike whenever she looked at him.

He tugged his hair free of the jacket collar and asked more abruptly than he intended, "What do you need?"

"What time is it?"

"Just after midnight."

"Have I been here a whole day, or just—?"

"About five hours," he said.

He could see her visibly relax, sinking back on her heels even more. "Thank goodness."

He remembered the picture in her wallet and the way she'd been looking at the man with her. Was he Jon? If that picture was the real thing no wonder she wanted to get out of here as soon as she could. "I think there's a chance you can get out of here in the morning." He saw her face light up with hope and he felt a stab of something he couldn't quite name when he saw how anxious she was to get to Jon. Either Jon was the luckiest man alive to have a woman like this love him, or this woman was a damned good actress.

He felt the dog nudge at his leg. "I'll be back in a bit," he murmured, then opened the door and stepped out into the light snow and wind. The moon was behind the clouds again, and it was hard to see very far into the night. That didn't stop the dog from darting out ahead of him, bounding off the porch, oblivious to everything.

"Damned animal," he muttered, and for the first time he wondered what the animal had been called by whoever owned him.

No. This dog wouldn't be "owned" by anyone. Not any more than Steven would be by another person. Steven never had been, and he never would be. And there would never be a woman like Alicia Sullivan trying to get to *him* in a damned blizzard. God, the woman almost died trying to get to her fiancé. *If* she had a fiancé. *If* she really was going to Harvester Road and not Harvester Road North. *If* she really loved the man in the picture.

As he ducked his head into the chill, he walked to the edge of the porch and jumped down into the knee-deep snow. Silently, he moved along the wall to the jutting rocks of the fireplace and the far window. He moved until he could see into the cabin through the narrow opening of the drapes.

He could see Alicia on the bed, just as he'd left her, and she was simply looking around the room. Then she moved, scrambling to the edge of the bed to get off. As she touched her feet to the carpet, she tossed the pillow back onto the bed, and he felt heat rush through him, despite the cutting cold in the air all around him.

He'd undressed her, put her in bed and lain next to her, but to see her standing there in an indecent excuse for lingerie was something else. He felt like a Peeping Tom, seeing the beauty of the woman secretly. Full breasts, the flare of slender hips, and long, shapely legs brought a response from him that was staggering.

For a moment she gripped the post of the bed to steady herself as if she was dizzy, the shirt pressed to her breasts. Then she let go of the bed, raked her wild hair back from her face with her free hand and walked slowly to the bathroom.

As she disappeared into the small room, Steven moved back and leaned against the wall. The chill was making his face begin to tingle, and he pushed his hands deep into his pockets for protection. He'd been alone too long, too cut off from people. From women. He must have seen many more beautiful women in his life, but he couldn't remember a single one right now. Not one with flaming curls, clear green eyes or legs that went on forever. And right then he knew what he'd felt back in the cabin just before he left. Jealousy.

The emotion was foreign to him. He had to be going stir-crazy if he could feel jealousy toward a man he didn't know over a woman he'd only met a few hours ago. She was a damned good actress or a woman in love. Maybe Alicia Sullivan was just illusion. He swiped at snow clinging to his face. Wasn't that what all of life was about . . . illusions? See what you wanted to see. Be who you wanted to be. Leave behind the past, the parts that didn't work out.

And his next illusion would begin after he'd testified against Shaw. He saw the dog not more than twenty feet from the cabin, standing chest-deep in snow, his coat being covered by the freshly falling flakes. The animal watched Steven from a distance, and seemed to be waiting for something.

Steven heard a door close in the cabin and moved back to look in the window. Alicia came out into the bedroom, thankfully wearing his shirt—although that was a mixed blessing. It covered her from her neck to her wrists and her thighs, but in some subtle way it was just as provocative as her near nakedness had been earlier. He saw her move slowly past the bed and into the living area.

Alicia wandered around the living room, holding her hands out to the fire, then turned and seemed to look right at the window. For a moment he thought she saw him, then she came toward the window and he knew what she was looking at. His books.

He didn't move, but as he watched Alicia, he thought about the end of Steven Rider. The man might fall off the face of the earth, but right then he decided it would be his own choice how and when it happened, not something Shaw would arrange.

Alicia stared at the closed door after Buck left. She suddenly felt extraordinarily weak and wondered if she had enough strength to even get off the bed. The idea of just lying down again and going to sleep was very tempting, but she knew before she could do that, she had to change. She couldn't sit here in her bra and panties forever.

Mustering up what strength she had, she awkwardly got off the bed, and for a moment the room spun. She grabbed the post of the bed and held on, the shirt clutched to her chest. And after a long moment, the world settled. Cautiously, she let go of her grip on the bed and made her way to the door Buck had motioned to.

As she opened it, she found a tiny bathroom. The door silently swung open and Alicia faced her own reflection in the mirror that hung over a freestanding sink across the room from her. Tangled hair, pale skin and no makeup. She looked like a waif. She moved inside and crossed the small room with its claw-footed tub and pull-chain commode. She laid the shirt on the edge of the tub, then turned on the tap in the sink and held her hands under it until the water ran warm over her skin.

She cupped her hands, caught water in them, then splashed it on her face. She picked up a small towel on a rack by the sink and buried her face in the white terry cloth. For a minute she didn't move, then she laid the towel on the side of the sink and reached for the shirt. She shook out the blue chambray, then put it on. It felt soft against her skin, and even though she was tall, Buck was even taller. The tails of the shirt touched her thighs, and the cuffs threatened to cover her hands. She rolled the sleeves up over her forearms, then looked at herself again.

Meeting her own shadowed gaze, she could see the tension at her eyes and mouth. She needed to get to Jon's as soon as she could. If she could get there tomorrow, maybe Ali and Lydia wouldn't have to know about this. There was no way she wanted to worry either of them. Lydia was doing well after her heart surgery, and Alicia had vowed she wouldn't give her any reason to worry. And Ali needed all her energy, both physically and emotionally, to get ready for the baby.

Alicia wasn't about to drag her sister into her mistakes again.

"Call Jack," she told her reflection. "Explain a bit of this to him and leave it up to him about how much or how little he wants to tell Ali and Lydia." That might be best. She sighed and leaned forward, resting her forehead against the coolness of the mirror, and she closed her eyes.

"I've given Ali and Lydia enough worry for one life. I don't want them to be drawn into this fiasco. One Mick Terrine experience in their lives was one too many." She drew back, combed her fingers through her curls and tucked them behind her ears, then turned and walked back into the bedroom area. She went past the bed and stepped into the living room.

She crossed the plank floor to the hearth, holding out her hands to the heat from the fire. As she glanced to her left, she saw the books on the desk by the window. She moved closer, seeing titles that ranged from techno-thrillers, to great literature, to a series on the history of Europe. And they all looked very new. As she turned, her toe struck something on the floor and she looked down at a book lying open facedown on the floor by the nearest leather chair. She stooped to pick it up and looked down at the title, a single word, *Fate*.

As she stared at the title, she began to dwell on the Fate at work in her own life. She knew the same Fate who had arranged to have George Terrine taken off this earth had arranged to have Buck find her. *Capricious* was a word that came to mind. It had got her out of one realm of danger and thrown her into another. And the worst part of all was she had no idea exactly where the new danger came from.

She didn't know if it came from Buck, or if it came from the suspicion that her old life and old ways weren't as far behind her as she'd thought they were by now.

Los Angeles

Ali put the phone down and turned to Jack, who was working at his desk in the small niche off the living room of the Victorian-style house they'd bought in the fall. The Christmas tree was still up, the presents gone, and the tiny twinkling lights made the room still feel festive.

"All the lines are down. No calls are going through to Gibson. Lydia's tried four times. No luck." She unconsciously rested her hand on her full stomach and slowly made circles on the soft fabric. "You don't think Alicia had trouble getting to Jon's, do you? The weather report said they're having a terrible storm up there."

Jack looked up from the files he was working on and sat back in the old swivel chair he'd brought from his apartment in Las Vegas. His good-luck chair, he'd called it, after he'd passed the California state bar exam. He fingered the scar on his chin and slowly smiled at Ali. That expression had made the world seem right in the middle of chaos back in Las Vegas over a year ago, and it was having the same effect on Ali now. "Alicia can take care of herself, sweetheart. You, of all people, should know that."

Ali wondered if she would ever get used to this feeling of not being alone, of being complete when Jack was with her. Two made one. Strange math, but a fact of her life. And with the baby, that two would soon be three, and they would still be one. It was awesome to her, and she found she had to blink rapidly to stop the tears that threatened.

All the hormones went crazy during pregnancy, she'd heard. They sure were with her. Maybe that was why she hadn't felt right since Alicia left for Colorado and why she'd needed to talk to her sister. "It's just that I..." She crossed to Jack as she tried to explain. "When she's gone, I don't know, I..."

Jack reached out to Ali and drew her down on his lap. His large hand touched her stomach and immediately the baby moved. "When she's gone, you feel as if you've lost her again, don't you?" he murmured.

He knew. He understood. She rested her head on his shoulder and loosely draped her arms around his neck. "Mind reader."

"Well, you haven't lost her. She's just gone to meet Jon's family. And if it works out, she'll get married to the man and be a happily married lady, just like you."

She drew back and met his gaze with mock surprise. "Me, a happily married lady?"

"Yes, you," he murmured, his voice catching as she dipped her head and touched her lips to the spot just under his ear. She could feel his pulse, the quickening of it against her lips. "You, you... are, aren't you?" he whispered, his voice growing unsteady.

"Yes, very," she sighed, loving the taste of him on her tongue as she undid two buttons on his shirt, just enough to slip her hand inside and touch the heat of his chest.

"Listen... Ali... we can't. Can we?"

"The doctor said to do everything I normally do until the last month, and..." She drew back enough to meet his gaze, the echo of her own needs showing deeply in his eyes. "I've got three more days before I'm into my ninth month."

"Three days?"

"Seventy-two hours."

His hand moved to cup her full breast, and she couldn't stop the moan of pleasure that came softly from her lips. "Work can wait," he whispered. "And you can call Ali later...tomorrow, or maybe on New Year's Eve, to wish her a happy New Year's."

She slipped off his lap, took his hand in both of hers and smiled at him. "You're right. My sister can take care of herself."

"Amen to that," Jack whispered and pulled Ali to him.

The longer Buck was gone, the more edgy Alicia got. Being alone was one thing, but being totally cut off from the world was something else. There were few sounds outside, and even fewer sounds in the cabin. She looked around for a television or radio, but couldn't see either one. A cursory glance showed no cigarettes, either. One thing to be thankful for. At least she didn't have to meet temptation head-on and fight it.

As she looked around, she realized something she hadn't been aware of until right then. There were no signs of the holidays in the cabin. No Christmas tree, no decorations and no sign there had ever been any. She stood in front of the fireplace and slowly turned, scanning the room. "Odd," she muttered to herself. "Unless he came here after Christmas."

And that brought the thought that she didn't even know if Buck lived here all the time or used it as a vacation house, if he owned it or rented it. She didn't know much at all about him except he'd saved her life and she'd been in his bed.

She laughed to herself as the thought struck her as funny. "I went to sleep in the snow, then woke up in the bed of a dark-haired man who is just about as disturbing as any man I've ever met. And as mysterious." With his slightly exotic looks and the tendency to show no emotion, she just wondered how he related to other people, to other women.

That sobered her. She knew how she'd reacted to him, and that bothered her a lot. "No more dangerous men for me," she muttered. "Give me a man like Jon, stable, decent, rich and..." Her voice trailed off and an uneasiness touched her when she realized the next word she was about to utter was "boring."

She shook her head sharply to banish that foolish notion and headed for the kitchen. "Ali likes him. Jack likes him. Lydia likes him." She stopped at the doorway and scanned the room. To her left was a small breakfast table and two chairs painted white. Straight across from the entry, the wall was filled with floor-to-ceiling cupboards with a small refrigerator set into a cubby-hole in the middle. Along the back wall, a single sink, tile counters and low cupboards sat under a window covered with beige curtains. Right by the door was a gas stove.

"Jon is perfect," Alicia muttered. "Just perfect."

Just as perfect as this room. Not a thing was out of order or jarring. "Jon isn't jarring," she said as she stepped into the kitchen and crossed to the cupboards.

As she opened door after door, she found that the interiors were just as perfect. "He's a bit opinionated, and he likes to have the last word, but he's not hard to be around." The cupboards were filled with neatly arranged cans, bottles, jars and containers of drinking water.

The one closest to the sink area had a set of glasses, plates and bowls. Everything looked as if it had never been disturbed. She turned and went to the refrigerator and opened it. It wasn't as full as the cupboards, but it contained plenty of food. "Eggs, bread, butter, fruit, milk, bottled water, beer." She smiled at a gigantic jar of peanut butter on the top shelf. "And enough peanut butter to feed a whole herd of elephants."

She took out a bottle of water, closed the refrigerator and walked back into the living area with the drink. As she sipped the water, she crossed to check her clothes on the hearth. "Still damp." She moved to the couch and sat down on the warm leather, tucking her feet under her. As she fingered the water bottle, she looked at the phone on the table next to the couch.

"Why not?" She reached for the receiver, then lifted it and listened. Nothing. Before she could put it back, she felt a prickling sensation course through her. Someone was watching her. She could feel eyes on her, that burning sensation of being observed.

She rested her water bottle on her thigh and slowly looked around, then behind her and around into the kitchen. No one was there. Nothing moved. Yet she could feel eyes on her.

"Nerves," she muttered to herself. "You're nervous. You almost died in the snow." She held tightly to the receiver still against her ear. "A stranger saves your life, and you get all kinds of weird ideas. No one's here except Buck and the dog. No one's watching you." Her own voice was a comfort in the stillness.

Slowly she replaced the receiver, then stood and drank down the last of the water. She turned to go back into the kitchen at the same time the front door opened. A billowing wind swept into the cabin as Buck came back inside, the dog ducking past him to go directly to the fire. Alicia felt real relief that Buck was back, until she looked into his eyes. His gaze was as unblinking and direct as ever, but there was an edge to it now, something she almost thought was anger. But why? Then she realized he didn't have any wood in his arms.

"Wasn't there any wood?" she asked.

He didn't respond at first, then he moved abruptly and shrugged out of his coat. He didn't speak until he shook the clinging snow off the leather, spotting the wooden floor with drops of moisture. After he hung the coat on a peg near the door, he turned back to Alicia and stepped out of his boots.

"I can't get the door to the shed open. We'll have to make do with what we have."

"Is there enough to last?"

"We'll make it last," he murmured as he kicked his boots against the wall by the door. Then he brushed past Alicia, and she caught the freshness of the night clinging to him, mingling with a scent that she could only call male. Quickly she stepped back and watched as he went to the phone, picked it up and listened. As he put the receiver back in place, he slanted a look at Alicia.

The tips of his fingers rested on the back of the receiver. "Was the phone just working?"

She shook her head. "No."

"Then who were you talking to?" he asked, his gaze never releasing hers.

Chapter 5

"Who was I talking to?" Alicia repeated. "What are *you* talking about?"

The tension in Buck was palpable. "I heard voices when I was coming in."

It suddenly dawned on her what he meant. "I was talking to myself," she admitted.

"You talk to yourself?" He looked as if he didn't quite believe her.

"Who did you think I was talking to?" She motioned to the room at large. "Do you see anyone else here, except you, me and the dog? And you and the dog were outside. I was talking to myself."

He drew his hand back from the phone. "You talk to yourself." A statement, not a question.

"Yes. It's a bad habit."

His frown didn't ease. "Is there anything else about you I should know about while you're here, any secrets or other strange behavior?"

The question seemed to echo from her past, and for a second she was in front of an evaluator for the foster care system. *"And is there anything else we should know about you, Alicia, before attempting placement in a foster home?"*

Sudden weakness robbed her of the ability to keep standing here facing this man, and she moved past him to go to the couch. As she sank down on the warm leather, she spoke without looking at Buck. "There is one other thing you should know about me."

"What?"

She watched pieces of wood fall off the burning logs, sending showers of sparks up the chimney. "I've been known to answer myself."

His rough chuckle startled her, and she darted a look at Buck, who had turned to face her. His hands were pushed into the pockets of his jeans and his hair fell darkly on the shoulders of his white shirt. What stopped her dead was the glint of real humor in his blue eyes.

"At least I'm forewarned," he said.

She wished she could smile, share in the first bit of humor there had been between them, but her lips felt stiff and unresponsive. All she could do was take in the fleeting change in Buck. For an instant he looked younger, maybe freer. And she had a glimpse of a man who could have stopped her in her tracks in any other situation.

Not now. Not when all he seemed to do was bring back emotions and feelings she thought she'd left behind years ago. She hated the memories of loneliness and being separated. She pushed her fingers through her thick hair and exhaled, needing the cleansing to help her think clearly. But before she had time to think of a reply, the dog came around the side of the couch and sank to his haunches beside her.

With a deep sigh, he laid his muzzle on her leg and rolled his eyes up at her. For one crazy moment, Alicia thought he understood the isolation she felt and was offering her some support. "Is this dog psychic?" she almost asked, but bit her lip to keep the words from being spoken. She didn't want to give Buck any more reasons to think she was crazy.

She rested her hand on the animal's head and felt the clinging dampness from the snow. Slowly, she stroked his fur and watched his eyes close with pleasure. He wanted contact, too, and in some way it soothed Alicia.

"Is one of your secrets that you're a witch?" Buck asked.

Alicia looked up at him and didn't find a trace of the humor that had been there before. His eyes were narrowed and totally unreadable. "What are you talking about?"

"You've obviously cast a spell on that animal. He never got that close to me, even when I fed him."

She almost said that Buck probably wouldn't have *let* the dog get this close even if the animal had tried. But she didn't. "He just wants to be petted."

He looked from Alicia to the dog, then turned and headed into the kitchen. "Are you hungry?" he called from the next room.

When she thought about it, she found that she was famished. "Yes, I am."

"Any preferences?" he called back.

Her vegetarian days were well behind her. "No, none," she said. "I'll eat anything except olives or sour cream."

"I don't have either one, so you're in luck. Keep the animal company, and I'll cook up something."

She felt the dog's ears twitch in the direction of Buck's voice, but he kept his head in her lap. "Maybe that's your problem," she called out to Buck.

"What's my problem?"

"I mean, that's why the dog doesn't make up to you. He's not just 'the animal.' He's got a soul, and you—"

Buck was back at the entrance to the kitchen, looking at her with a frown. "What in the hell are you talking about?"

"You said he doesn't come to you for petting. It's because you make him feel like he's a thing instead of being a—"

"Correct me if I'm wrong, but last time I looked, he was a dog. That means he's an animal."

"And you're a man, but you've got a name. It's not right that he's just called 'the dog' or 'the animal.'"

His frown deepened with impatience. "Then give him a damned name, if you want. I'm sure it won't make a bit of difference to him, but if it makes you feel better, then go ahead and—"

"How do you know it won't make a difference?" she asked, cutting off his words.

"How do you know it will?" he countered.

She knew. She remembered. "Alicia," she'd yelled at one of her foster mothers when the woman had called her the "new kid." "My name's Alicia, Alicia, Alicia!" She looked away from Buck, back to the dog and murmured, "I know he needs a name."

The dog's deep brown eyes gazed up at her, looking for all the world as if he knew the secret of peace. A flight of fancy, probably, but it made her feel better just to stroke his head and feel the weight of his muzzle on her thigh.

"Well, what's it going to be?" Buck asked.

She was blank for a moment. "Excuse me?"

"The name—what's it going to be?"

The perfect name came to her. "Pax. I'll call him Pax. It's Latin for peace."

"Latin? I'm impressed."

"Don't be too impressed. I had half of a semester of Latin in high school. I dropped out when I knew I was going to fail, but that word stuck for some reason." She ruffled the dog's fur with her fingers. "He looks as if he's at peace with himself, doesn't he?"

"He looks as if he's got your number," Buck muttered, then changed the subject. "How about chili and toast?"

"That's fine."

"Good, because there isn't much of a choice."

"You've got a cupboard full of food," she said as she looked back at him.

She didn't miss the way his mouth tightened, but his tone gave away little. "You've taken inventory?"

"I'm sorry. I was looking around while you were out getting the wood, and your cupboard is far from empty.'' She found a slight smile. ''And you'll never run out of peanut butter.''

His expression didn't change. ''So, you checked out everything?''

''I'm sorry,'' she muttered, hating the way he could put her on the defensive seemingly without trying. ''I didn't think your cupboards were top secret.''

''I didn't say they were,'' he said and turned from her to head for the kitchen. ''Keep the animal company, and I'll get the food.''

''Pax. His name is Pax,'' she called after him, and she felt the dog twitch his ears. He knew his name already.

When Buck ignored her and kept going, Alicia patted the dog, then eased back and got to her feet to hurry after Buck. How long had she known this man—maybe an hour all told since she'd been awake, or six hours if you counted the five she was unconscious. She didn't understand how he could affect her so easily in so short a time.

She stopped in the doorway to the kitchen, and she saw Buck taking two large cans of chili from the cupboard along with some seasoning and a bottle of hot sauce. He put them on the stove top, then pulled open a side drawer and took out a can opener. She touched the rough log wall by the door, weakness in her legs making her take the support.

The wall felt rough and solid, helping Alicia get centered. Overreacting was something she'd been good at in the past, but she'd learned that control was far better. And it was more acceptable, especially when she was face-to-face with someone who had saved her life. She took a breath and spoke as evenly as possible.

"I'm sorry I looked in your refrigerator and cup-boards, and I know you think it's foolish to give the dog a name."

When he didn't respond and kept opening the cans, she found herself speaking quickly. "I just sort of barged in here, and it's obvious that you like being alone, so I apologize for intruding. I know I'd hate it if I wanted to be alone and someone tried to die in my front yard and I had to put them in my bed, and..."

Her voice trailed off. That was the last thing she wanted to think about now—being in this man's bed. She bit her lip as Buck looked at her, his gaze partially obscured for a moment by his dark hair and narrowed eyes. Then he tucked his hair behind his ears and she caught the full impact of his direct gaze. "How hot you like your chili?" he asked. "Boring, interesting or ex-citing?"

She had a disturbing feeling he could have inserted the word "men" for "chili" and had a valid question for her. And there was no doubt where this man would fit. "Exciting," she murmured.

"I thought so." He opened the oven door on the stove and took out a large pan, then set it on the stove and poured the cans of chili into it. As he tipped a healthy shot of hot sauce into the chili, Alicia tried to think of something to say. Something safe.

"So, where are you from, Buck?"

He stirred the chili, then flicked the burner under the pot on high. "All over," he said.

She watched him take the empty chili cans and drop them in a wastebasket under the sink. "So, this isn't your permanent home?"

He turned to her and leaned back against the sink. He took his time crossing his arms on his chest, his blue eyes inscrutable. "No, it's a . . ." He exhaled. "I guess you'd call it a vacation place."

"You own it?"

"No, I'm renting."

"Where did you spend Christmas?"

"Here."

"But..." She drew her hand back from the wall and echoed his stance, crossing her arms on her breasts. "I mean, there aren't any decorations or anything."

He shrugged, a sharp motion of his broad shoulders that tugged at the confines of his cotton shirt. "I'm not big on holidays. They come and go. I don't notice."

"Even Christmas?"

"Even Christmas."

"How about the Fourth of July? Or Easter? Or New Year's?"

"What about them?" he asked.

"I always thought they were magical, a time when anything was possible."

"I found out a long time ago that was all a bunch of bull." He went back to the stove, picked up a wooden spoon and began to stir the chili. "A day is just a day. Just because someone makes it a national holiday doesn't make it anything more than an excuse to take off work."

"Obviously you're off work," she said, with what she thought was excellent logic.

He didn't stop stirring the chili. "How would you know that?"

That took her aback. "Aren't you off work? Or do you work here?"

"No, I don't work here. And me being here has nothing to do with the holidays."

"So, what kind of work do you do?"

He slanted her a quick look, then went back to studying the circles he was stirring in the thick chili. "Odds and ends. Whatever comes along. What do you do for money?"

"I work in a travel agency. Do you ski?"

"What does that have to do with anything?"

"I was just wondering why you're here."

He stopped stirring and looked right at her. The question had been something to say, to fill the uncomfortable void she sensed when they weren't talking. But he seemed to tense, and his eyes narrowed. "What difference does it make?"

"None at all," she muttered, at a loss to know what to say to this man. He gave away nothing about himself, and was so closed she felt as if she was almost alone. "Not any more than how you feel about the holidays makes any difference. It's just sort of sad, and I—"

She'd done it again. She knew she'd said the wrong thing when he dropped the spoon against the side of the pot and took one step toward her. "Do me a favor, Miss Sullivan?"

"Sure, of course," she said quickly, fighting the urge to take a step herself—backward.

"Stop telling me that what I think or believe is sad."

"But, I don't—"

"Oh, yes, you do. It's sad that I didn't give the damn animal a name, and it's sad that I 'bah humbug' Christmas and that I don't shoot off rockets on the Fourth of July. Get this straight. It's not sad, it's just the way I feel and the way I do things. I've got a right to feel any way I want to feel. Agreed?''

She felt dizzy from the feelings he could create in her with a word or a look, and from the speed that they came and went. The old Alicia came from nowhere, and she found herself squaring to face him directly and look him right in the eyes. "Agreed. You do. And I've got a right to feel any way I want to feel. And I happen to feel that it's sad that you can have a dog and not give it a name, and that you could make Scrooge look like the Good Fairy!"

Before she could do more than drag air into her tight lungs, Buck took another step toward her, his blue eyes riveting her to the spot, and the buffer of space between them was cut to mere inches. "I've never cared what anyone thought about me, and I don't give a damn what you think about me, lady. Tomorrow you'll go back to your upper-middle-class celebrations, and you have my blessings to do it."

"And you can get back your isolation," she said through clenched teeth.

She heard the harsh release of air at the same time she felt the heat of his breath brush her face. For a moment she braced herself, certain he was going to come even closer, but he didn't. He turned from her, went back to the stove and picked up the spoon again. He methodically began stirring the chili again, not saying a word. But Alicia could see the way the muscle in his jaw was working. Control. He had it in spades.

Pax pushed his head against Alicia's bare leg to let her know he was there, and he let out a low whining sound. When she dropped her hand to touch his head, the sound stopped, but he kept up the pressure against her leg with his shoulder. She knew he hated what was happening as much as she did. And something foreign came to her. She wanted to apologize. She seldom did that. Ali had told her it wasn't in her basic makeup. Something omitted from her DNA structure.

Yet, as she watched Buck, she knew she should apologize. Fighting with a man who had saved your life was stupid, and arguing with this man was ridiculous. It was downright ungrateful. And she was very grateful to not be lying dead in the snow right now.

She almost stepped toward him and touched his arm to get his attention, but realized that contact was the last thing he wanted with her. "Buck, I—"

Her words were cut off by a low rumbling sound. Then the cabin began to tremble as if a giant hand had closed over it and was shaking it up and down and from side to side.

Alicia stared at Buck in horror. It was an earthquake.

Pax let out an eerie howl, and Buck muttered a low curse as he grabbed Alicia by the upper arm. "Let's get the hell out of here," he said, and the next thing she knew, she was being pulled into the living room and toward the front door.

"No! Stop!" she gasped, but Buck kept going, taking her with him. The dog howled; the rumbling seemed to be everywhere, and the tiny cabin shook.

When Buck got to the door, Alicia knew she wasn't going outside. This crazy man could, but she wasn't going anywhere. Not in an earthquake, and not with the possibility that one of those huge trees she remembered from before could come crashing down on her.

She dug in and managed to stammer, "S-stop!" and in the next second, everything did stop, as if she had commanded it.

The cabin stilled, the rumbling faded off into the distance, the dog fell silent, and Buck froze with a hand on the doorknob, the other still holding on to Alicia. "I don't—"

His grip on her tightened, stopping her words. "Quiet. Don't move," he whispered.

She didn't move or speak until Buck released a harsh breath. "I think it's done," he murmured.

Alicia had been shocked by the earthquake, but what was even more disturbing right now was this man holding on to her. She could feel his fingers on her as clearly as if her skin had been bare. The heat of his body radiated through the cotton of the shirt she was wearing, and when his hold on her relaxed a bit, she pulled free.

Her knees felt weak, and she reached out to steady herself by gripping the back of the nearest chair. She looked up at Buck, and she didn't know just how unsettled she was by everything until she tried to speak. She could hear the tinge of hysteria in her voice. "Don't you know you're supposed to get in a doorway when there's an earthquake? You don't go running outside where God-knows-what could fall on you. Like those trees, or the cabin walls or the chimney. You get under a heavy table or in a doorway, but you don't go outside. That's just common sense, for heaven's sake!"

Buck pressed one hand flat against the closed door and glared at her until she finished, then he spoke.

"And common sense tells you when there's an avalanche you run like hell in the opposite direction."

She swallowed hard. "No, that wasn't..."

"It sure was. And with any luck, we aren't buried under tons of snow."

She clenched her fingers on the back of the chair and felt a trembling in her legs. "An avalanche?" she whispered.

"Exactly," he said as he stood straight, grabbed the doorknob and pulled the barrier back.

Cold air flooded into the cabin, making Alicia's trembling increase and her head grow light. She swallowed hard as Buck turned to look outside. The light-headedness was turning to a fuzzy, soft feeling of being spiraled upward. Buck was speaking, his words a blur in her ears, and she let go of the chair, knowing it wasn't enough of an anchor to keep her earthbound.

She needed something more. Buck. He could keep her anchored. She reached out for him, but before she could touch him, the world turned gray, and she floated off into nothingness.

Steven could almost be thankful for an avalanche if it stopped the arguing. Maybe it was the flame-colored hair, or maybe it was a result of his edginess in not knowing just who she was or why she was here, but he didn't seem to be capable of saying a thing right when he was with Alicia. Surprisingly, it made his insides knot. Usually he didn't give a damn if he got along with anyone. And he wasn't comfortable with it now.

The front of the cabin was clear except for the heavily falling snow, and he guessed that the avalanche was a short way off. They were safe for now. He spoke as he turned back to Alicia. "That's a relief, but I'd better check out..." He was braced for the next clash, but his words died out.

She was by the chair, one hand slowly lifting, then her eyes fluttered and rolled upward, all color drained from her face, and she pitched forward. Steven moved instinctively, reaching out, catching her before she could collapse on the floor. He had her in his arms, cradling her to his chest, and his heart raced. As unprepared as he'd been for her collapsing, he was even more unprepared for the fear that shot through him.

She was limp, barely breathing, and he cursed the fact that the phone was out. When Pax began to whine, it only added to his raw nervousness. Quickly, he carried Alicia to the bed and laid her down on the linen. When the dog would have climbed right up by her, Steven held out his hand to stop him.

"Not this time," he said, blocking him. The dog stopped, looked at Steven, then circled to the far side of the bed and rested his muzzle on the edge of the mattress. Silently, he watched Alicia.

"Damn dog, you'd think you were human," Steven muttered as he sank down on the bed and touched Alicia on the cheek. He wasn't a doctor. He could take care of himself, but taking care of her was something entirely different.

Maybe it was a delayed reaction to the experience in the snow. Or maybe he'd upset her by arguing with her. Damn it, he wished he knew what was going on. He touched her throat, found her pulse and felt a degree of relief to feel the beat was strong and steady. He trailed his fingertips along her jawline, then touched her cheek with the palm of his hand. Her skin looked more normal with color returning to it and there was no fever. That meant no infection. He knew that much.

He felt her stir, then her eyes fluttered, her lashes dark against her skin, and she moaned. The dog immediately looked up, his head cocked to one side, one ear straight up.

"Alicia?" Steven said, bending closer, gently brushing at the curls that clung to her forehead. "Alicia? Wake up. That's it. Just open your eyes. Alicia, open your eyes."

How could she be such a spitfire one minute and look so incredibly delicate and vulnerable the next? The woman was a mystery to him in more ways than one. "Alicia," he said again, and this time she responded.

Her eyes fluttered again and slowly opened, their deep green unfocused for a moment, then her gaze sharpened. Color touched her cheeks and her bottom lip trembled. "Wh-what happened?" she whispered hoarsely, struggling to raise herself on her elbows.

He touched her shoulders, easing her back on the bed, and the unsteadiness he felt under his hands made his heart catch. "You passed out."

She sank back on the pillow and closed her eyes as she exhaled. "I can't believe it. I've never fainted in my life, but now I..." She bit her lip. "First you dig me out of the snow, then you find out I've got the vapors. I'm getting to be a real pain for you, aren't I?"

He couldn't begin to define just what she was becoming for him. "The vapors?" he asked, trying to make his mouth lift in a smile. "What are they?"

Her hand fell back on to the pillow above her head, and she opened her eyes, her gaze veiled by her long lashes. "Vapors. Ladies of refinement used to have the vapors on a regular basis. I think it was because they had their corsets tied too tightly, but they dropped like flies."

His smile came easier as she spoke. "Cuts off the oxygen, I guess."

"And the circulation. I don't know why I'd faint like that."

"You've been through a hell of a lot, even an avalanche."

She paled when he said that. "Are we . . ."

"We're fine. We're not buried. But it's snowing like crazy again. There must have been a buildup on one of the nearby slopes and it simply broke off." He stood and looked down at her.

As he met her veiled gaze, he wondered when vulnerability in a woman had become an aphrodisiac for him. All she had to do was look at him like that, and he knew that at another time, in another place, he would have done his level best to know her on every imaginable level.

But this wasn't the time or the place. "Are you still hungry?"

"I think so."

The dog whined, and she looked at him. "Pax?" She reached out and touched his head as he settled his muzzle on the bed again. "I bet you're sick of me, too," she said as her fingers stroked his fur.

Steven watched her, the way she touched the dog, gently ruffling his fur, and the way she talked in a soft, soothing voice to the animal. Jealousy of a man was one thing, but he was beginning to feel a certain degree of jealousy for the dog being on the receiving end of this woman's affection.

"I'll get you some food," he muttered and turned away from the bed to go to the kitchen. With a wall between them and the distractions of making a meal, he could get his bearing and get a grip on reality.

Jaimie L. was to meet his Houston connection at a souvenir stand in the airport in Seattle. He had his ticket bought, a one-way flight to Chicago, via Denver, and he stood by the magazine rack, flipping through a home improvement book while he watched for Shaw's man to arrive.

One minute after the agreed-upon meeting time, Shaw's man entered the store. A big, burly man who looked as if he had "bodyguard" written all over him. He was all in black, wearing a fedora and carrying a slim briefcase under one arm.

Jaimie L. made eye contact, then motioned across to the rest rooms. Shaw's man lifted an eyebrow in acknowledgment, then went first. Jaimie L. followed him. Inside, the two men went through the motions of using the facilities, then both approached the sinks. Shaw's man put the slim briefcase he was carrying on the side of the sink, then washed his hands.

Jaimie L. ran the water over his hands, never looking at the other man, then, as he flipped off the faucet, he grabbed a paper towel. He glanced in the mirrors, saw Shaw's man watching him, and he smiled.

"Traveling gets old, doesn't it?" he said.

The man nodded. "You've got that right. Real old."

"Where're you from?" Jaimie L. asked.

"Texas. On my way back. How about you?" he asked as he reached for a paper towel. "Where are you from?"

"Colorado—a small town called Gibson."

"Never heard of it," the man muttered and tossed the towel into the wastebasket. "Are you going there now?"

"Yeah, I'll get there…" He flipped off the water and glanced at his watch. 1:00 a.m. "In about eight hours."

"That sounds good," the man said, then brushed past Jaimie L., heading for the door. "Have a good ride," he said and went out the door.

Jaimie L. turned to the mirror and smiled at himself. "Yeah, I'll have a good ride," he murmured, then reached for the briefcase the man had left.

He felt the weight of the money in it, then tucked it under his arm and left the rest room. As he stepped out into the crowded terminal, he looked around for a gift shop. He had an hour before his flight took off. Now that the Rider hit was on track, he wondered if he had enough time to pick up a souvenir for his wife.

Chapter 6

By the time Steven came back into the room carrying a tray with two bowls of chili, two glasses of milk and some buttered toast, Alicia was sitting up in bed. She'd pushed pillows behind her back, and the dog was stretched out by her side on top of the comforter. His tail made lazy side-to-side motions as Alicia talked softly and patted his head.

Steven crossed to the bed. "Get down," he said, the command making both the dog and Alicia dart a startled look at him. But the dog didn't move.

"Get off the bed," he said, but the only reaction he got from the dog was a lifted eyebrow.

"I said to get—"

"Down, Pax," Alicia cut in and pointed to the floor with her left hand. "Down."

The dog moved immediately and jumped off the bed. Then he sat on the side farthest from Steven and rested his chin on the sheets, his unblinking gaze pinning Steven.

"That's just great," Steven muttered as he laid the tray on the bed beside Alicia.

"Pardon me?" she said, reaching for the nearest bowl of chili and a spoon.

"He's a stubborn son of a—" Steven bit off his words and sat on the edge of the bed, careful not to jar the tray. "Forget it. Eat up while it's hot."

"Maybe if you called him by his name, he'd pay attention to you," Alicia said as she stirred her chili.

"I hate to tell you this, but he wouldn't know the difference if you called him a tree."

Her spoon stilled, and her green eyes met his gaze. "Do you really believe that?"

"Sure."

"Then do it."

"Do what?"

She put the chili bowl back on the tray and sat against the pillows, her arms crossed on her breasts. "Call him a tree and get him to come to you."

"No, I'm not—"

"Do it. Prove it."

"I don't have to prove anything to anyone. The animal isn't—"

"You know that animals have souls, don't you?"

He couldn't follow any of this. "What are you talking about?"

"Souls. The seat of your affection. It's where you feel good or bad or happy or sad. People have souls and so do dogs."

"Dogs have fleas," he muttered and reached for his food. "The chili's getting cold."

"You're a total cynic, aren't you?" she asked as she picked up her chili again.

"Probably." He tasted the chili before he looked back at Alicia. "And I don't want to have to repeat this—it's my business if I'm a cynic."

"It certainly is," she said, but it was said too easily. He waited for the smart retort. But it didn't come. She ate in silence, casting him an unreadable look once or twice, but that was it.

"Go ahead, say it," he finally said.

She stopped with a spoonful of chili halfway to her mouth. "Say what?"

"That you think it's sad that I'm a cynic."

"I didn't say that." She ate the spoonful of chili, then drank some milk. As she put the glass back on the tray, she met his gaze. "But, if the shoe fits . . ."

"You've got milk on your upper lip," he muttered, "and the shoe doesn't fit."

She smiled, a gentle curve of her lips, and reached for the napkin. "I bet it fits you real well," she murmured, then wiped her mouth.

Steven didn't know how to react. Anger wasn't an option, not when she was sitting in his bed, looking for all the world like Little Orphan Annie, and not when she was smiling like that. "Eat your food," he muttered and looked away from her to eat his chili.

He was surprised at the hunger in him. He hadn't been this hungry all the time he'd been at the cabin. A peanut butter sandwich or snacks had done him just fine. As he put down the empty chili bowl and reached for a piece of toast, he looked at Alicia.

Her chili bowl was almost empty, and she was watching him with those incredible eyes. "Do you want more?" he asked.

"No, thanks." She put her bowl back on the tray and picked up the glass of milk. She drank the last of it, then slowly ran her tongue over her upper lip. "I'm full, but that was great."

As she reached out to put the milk back on the tray, Steven took the glass from her. For an instant, his fingers brushed hers and an electrical shock, which couldn't have been more stunning if it had come from a bolt of lightning, shot through him. Quickly, he pulled back and put the glass on the tray.

When he looked at Alicia, she was smiling the way she had been earlier. Arguing kept things square, as far as he was concerned. When they argued, he could remember that she might be an employee of Shaw's. But when she smiled, he couldn't think of much past the fact that when she left tomorrow, he'd never forget she'd been here.

He looked away and stood, picking up the tray. "I'll take this out and be right back." Hopefully when he got back, the smile would be gone and he could think clearly.

But when he stepped back into the bedroom area five minutes later, only part of his wish had come true. The smile was gone, but he couldn't think clearly at all. Alicia was resting against the headboard, the comforter up to her waist, her hair loose and brilliant against the white of the pillowcase.

As he neared the bed, he asked, "How are you feeling?"

"Better, thanks."

Steven realized the dog wasn't by the bed, and he saw the animal was curled up in front of the fireplace. "What's he doing over there?"

"Resting. He knows everything's all right, and he's taking a break."

Was she serious? He looked back at her and knew she was, but he wasn't about to start a debate with her right now. She was an odd woman, but fascinating. "Answer me something?"

She cocked her head to one side, sending him a considering glance. "That all depends on what the question is."

"I just wondered why you talked to yourself."

"I don't really talk to myself. I just think out loud. I was alone a lot when I was growing up, and I got in the habit."

He doubted that a woman who looked like Alicia would ever be alone for long. "What about your family?"

"I've got one sister. But we were separated a lot."

"What about your parents?"

"They died when I was five."

Steven sat down on the edge of the bed. "I'm sorry."

"It's okay." She looked past him to some spot near the fireplace. "I've had a long time to get used to the idea."

You could get used to a lot of things if you had enough time. He knew that better than most. "But you had your sister."

"Sometimes. There wasn't any other family, so there wasn't anyone to take my sister and me in. So we ended up getting shuffled into the foster-care system in L.A.

county, and sometimes we got separated. Sometimes we got to be together. Then things were pretty good.''

He could hear the studied casualness in Alicia's voice, but it couldn't hide the hint of pain that shadowed her eyes. If he had to bet, he'd bet she was telling the truth, at least about her background. And he was surprised at the stab of sympathy he felt for what Alicia must have gone through when she was a child.

His life had been different. His mother had never been there for him even when she was alive. And he'd *chosen* to leave his old life behind. That was worlds away from having everything snatched away from you. Sympathy or empathy had never been one of his strong suits, yet he could almost swear he knew the pain she must have felt. ''How long were you in foster homes?''

''Until I was twelve.'' Her face softened, and a smile that was slight, but so deep in her eyes that it made his heart lurch, played around the corner of her lips. ''Then Lydia and Harry Barrows took us in, and we had a family.''

''They adopted you?''

''No, they never did. They said we should have our own names, but they made us part of their family. They didn't have a lot of money, but one Fourth of July they rented this little cottage on the beach in Mexico.''

He was taken aback to see her eyes become overly bright with what might have been threatening tears. He didn't understand. ''It didn't turn out well?''

''Oh, it was wonderful. The fireworks were terrific and the weather was really balmy. It was perfect. We were a real family.'' She nibbled on her bottom lip. ''Three months later, Harry died. He had a heart attack. You know, I think it was worse when Harry died than when my parents did. He was terrific.''

She sat forward, pulling her legs up to cross them under the comforter and lean toward Steven. "He used to dress up like Santa on Christmas, even though we were teenagers. 'You got to believe in fantasy,' he used to say. And one year he dressed up like the Easter bunny.''

This close, Steven was bombarded by a gentle fragrance that seemed to cling to Alicia even though she was in his shirt and in his bed. He steeled himself. "So that's why you're so big on holidays?''

She shrugged, a fluttery movement of her shoulders under his shirt. "I guess so. It's just the memories are so special.'' She rocked slowly back and forth. "You know, someday I'd like to get back there, to Mexico.'' She smiled again, a wistful expression that seemed to gentle the world. "Strange how you can remember things so clearly, just out of the blue like that.''

"Memory is a strange thing.''

She nodded her head, making her hair fall forward over her shoulders. "You're right. I don't remember my parents very much. Just that my mother had red hair and a soft, soft voice. My father was tall, really tall, and he rode me on his shoulders. But I don't remember what color his hair was. That's strange, isn't it?''

If someone had told him this morning that he'd be having a philosophical conversation with a beautiful titian-haired woman in his bed tonight, he would have thought they were mad. "The human mind is selective in what it retains. Good and bad. They say you forget the good and the bad with equal ease. Or remember it the same way."

"What do you remember about your childhood?" she asked, jolting him with the question.

"Not much."

"Are your parents still alive?"

"The last time I heard, my father was. My mother died when I was thirteen." He'd never realized how bleak that sounded until now.

"You don't see your father?"

"No. I haven't since I was sixteen."

He could see the questions in her eyes before they found their way to her lips. If she was playing a part, she was doing a remarkable job of making him think she was a woman with a face as readable as a neon sign. One thing he knew for sure. He didn't want those questions to come from her.

The dog got up from his place in front of the fireplace and came over to the bed...on the side away from Steven. The dog glanced at Steven, then moved closer to Alicia and licked his lips. "All right," Steven muttered and got to his feet. "I hope the animal likes chili."

"You can't feed a dog chili," Alicia said. "Don't you have something better, like meat or dog food?"

"He showed up here uninvited, so I had no idea I'd need dog food. And there's no corner store to go to right now."

"How about eggs? You've got eggs, and dogs like them. I could cook them for him."

"No. I don't want you to fall over again. Chili will do for him. If he doesn't like it, I'm sure he'll come in and tell you all about it."

She smiled at that, but he could see the heaviness of sleep in her eyes. "Do you think I can communicate with him telepathically?"

"Probably."

"I'm not a witch," she said, the smile that was still intact revealing a tiny dimple to the right of her mouth. "I just like animals. I never had a dog. You know, moving around so much, then Harry was allergic, and Lydia never had pets. She called Harry her pet." She sank back in the pillows, looking up at him from under those ridiculously long lashes. "Did you have a dog when you were a kid?"

"No, I didn't."

"Then we were both deprived. But you're lucky. You've got Pax."

"He goes with the cabin. When I'm out of here, he's staying. He can bug the next renter."

"You can't mean that," she said, sitting up straight, a frown tugging a fine line between her eyes. "Just like that, you'd leave him?"

"He managed before me, and he'll manage fine after I leave."

"I don't think you mean that."

"I mean it."

"No, you couldn't. If you were that sort of person, you would have left me in the snow to die. But you didn't. You didn't walk away."

But he'd have to walk away from her, and that time would be here soon. "He's a dog, not a human being."

"But he's got—"

"I know. He's got a soul. And you look exhausted. I'm not going to argue about this now. Trust me, he'll be here long after I'm gone."

"When are you leaving?"

Her eyes looked so guileless, yet he could feel himself tightening at the question. "Why?"

She looked taken aback. "I was just asking."

"My plans are fluid. I don't know when I'll leave." He started for the kitchen and tossed over his shoulder, "I'll feed the animal."

"His name is Pax," she called after him. "Pax."

"All right, all right," he called back, and as he reached for the dog's dish from under the sink, he heard the dog come into the kitchen. He turned, looked at the animal and almost laughed. "So, if I give you food, you'll come, is that it? You're a true mercenary."

The dog cocked his head to one side and sat down on the brown tile. Steven put some chili in the dish, then hunkered down to hold it out to the dog. "Here you go." The animal didn't move. "Come on. You're the hungry one," he muttered and put the dish on the floor.

The dog looked at the dish, then back to Steven. "Food," Steven said, pointing to the dish. Nothing. He rocked back on his heels, eyed the dog, then said, "Food... Pax."

The animal got up and came over to the dish. Without a glance at Steven, he started to eat. Steven shook his head, then stood and went around the dog to go back into the other room. "That dog is pure crazy," he said as he came around the corner and stepped up into the bedroom area. "He's got a real attitude, and I..."

His voice trailed off when he saw Alicia had slid down in the bed and turned onto her side. Her eyes were closed, her hair tangled around her face and her hands folded under her cheek. She was asleep. Steven went closer and bent down to tug the comforter up to her shoulders.

His hand lingered on the deep blue cover, and he wondered when things had changed. This place was a haven, a place he chose to stay in to be safe until they called him for testimony. Yet, looking down at Alicia, he knew that when she left, he'd miss her. He'd miss the arguments, the strange things she'd said, the talking to herself, the way she had with the dog, and the sight of her.

He drew back. No, that was crazy. *She's beautiful, sexy, smart. That's it.* Yet, watching her in sleep could become an obsession with him. His hands closed into fists at his side. And she could have been sent to kill him. He turned from the sight of her, from a peace that seemed to cling to her that made him ache. And he wasn't at all sure why.

Alicia came out of sleep abruptly—one minute she was drifting in soft comfort, the next she was conscious of being in the huge four-poster bed...alone. She wasn't waking to Buck holding her this time. There was no heat pressed to her side, no heart beating under her cheek. She rolled onto her back, opening her eyes while she stretched her arms over her head and pointed her toes to the footboard.

She stared at the beamed ceiling and wondered where Buck had slept. She knew if he'd been in the bed, she would remember. She'd never forget the first time he shared her bed. "Enough of this," she muttered and sat up. As soon as the plows came through, she could get out of here and go to Jon's. And Buck would be more than glad to see her gone.

She tugged her legs to her chest and wrapped her arms around them. With her chin resting on her knees, she looked around. "Buck? Pax?" She couldn't hear anything in the bathroom. Then she realized the curtains on the windows that flanked the fireplace had been pulled back. The panes of glass were opaque with frost, but there was daylight outside, cool and blue.

Her clothes were still laid on the raised hearth, and a glance at the coat rack by the door showed that Buck's jacket was gone. He must have gone outside for wood. "Now's my chance to take a shower and get back in my own clothes." She scrambled out of bed, and as her feet hit the floor, she realized how much better she felt. The weakness was gone, her head was clear, and her legs were steady. She padded barefoot to the hearth, picked up her slacks and sweater, then crossed to the bathroom.

When she stepped into the small room, it was still steamy with the lingering heat and moisture from a recent shower. The mellow scent of after-shave hung in the air. A toothbrush and double-edged razor were on the side of the sink, and a towel had been discarded on the back of the toilet.

Buck had been in here recently, and the room seemed to be filled with his essence. She closed the door and turned on the water in the tub. As the tub filled with steamy water, she took off Buck's shirt and noticed the bottom button was missing. She couldn't remember if it had been there when she put on the shirt or not. For a moment she held the blue cotton, then dropped it over the towel on the back of the toilet.

As she turned to the tub, she caught a glimpse of herself. Her hair was mussed, the natural curl wild and untamed. Without a bit of makeup left, her skin looked pale, her eyes shadowed and the few freckles she had on her nose seemed prominent. If she walked in on Jon's family looking like this, they'd probably send her back out into the snow.

She smiled at that thought, until the memory of trudging through the storm yesterday came to her. Being surrounded by that fatal warmth was something she'd never forget. She trembled and turned from her image. She owed Buck her life. It was that simple. And she intended to make it up to him someway.

When Alicia came out of the bathroom fifteen minutes later, the cabin was still empty. In her sweater and corduroy slacks, she felt more normal, knowing if she looked in a mirror, she'd see Alicia Sullivan, not some waif in a stranger's shirt.

She felt her stomach rumble and almost went into the kitchen to see if she could find something to eat, but she remembered when Buck had found out that she'd gone through the cupboards before. No, she'd wait for him to come back, then she could eat. She didn't want to do anything else to make him angry. No more fights. No more words. She just wanted to thank him, and leave on a good note.

She glanced at the bed, at the linens that were bunched and mussed. One thing she could do was make the bed. She moved around, smoothing the sheets, tucking them in at the foot of the bed. She went around to tuck in the sides, first the one on the bathroom side, then she circled the bed to the far side. With both hands, she pushed the linen between the mattress and box spring.

Her fingers hit against something under the mattress, and she pushed her hand in farther. She could feel something cold and hard, and she caught it between her forefinger and thumb, then tugged. When a gun came slipping out from under the mattress, she gasped, "Oh, heavens."

Cautiously, she held the handgun up and stared at it. She'd never touched a gun before. She'd never wanted to, and this gun looked particularly lethal. It wasn't a gun that had a barrel with bullets in it. It was squared off, about eight inches from front end to back, and the grip was worn leather that had been tooled with an initial that could have been an *R* or maybe a *B* for Buck. She couldn't really tell.

It was scary holding something that could take a life, and she gingerly shifted it until she had it by the handle, pointing it at the floor. A safety. She'd heard about that, something that would keep the gun from firing, but she had no idea what a safety would even look like. And the way her luck was going lately, she'd probably fire the gun and shoot herself in the foot if she touched anything.

What she wanted to know was why Buck had a gun under his mattress. "Just ask him," she told herself. "When he comes in, give it to him and ask what it's all about. Until then, put it away."

She was just about to push it back under the mattress, when she heard a noise and started to turn, but

never got a chance to do it. She was blindsided by
weight and strength. The gun flew out of her hand, and
she was thrown onto the bed.

Chapter 7

All Steven saw, when he opened the door to the cabin, was Alicia by the bed with a gun in her hand. Every suspicion and fear he'd had since he'd found her in the snow came into focus, and he acted on raw adrenaline. She was working for Shaw. She'd been sent to kill him.

In a heartbeat, he closed the distance between himself and Alicia, and as she turned to aim the gun at him, he hit her and hit her hard. The gun went to the right, and the weight of his body carried Alicia onto the bed.

Her scream tore through the room, then he was tangled in the sheets with her under him, fighting him with a strength that shocked him. She twisted and threw her head from side to side, whipping her hair back and forth until it stung his forearms and face. Her foot struck him squarely on his shin, then her hands went for his face. Before he could stop her, the heel of her hand jabbed his chin, pressing his head back.

He'd never fought a woman. The thought made him sick. He'd seen enough damage done to a woman by a man when he'd been small, but this went past man and woman. Alicia was fighting as if he was going to kill *her,* and the bottom line was, he would if he had to.

He snapped his forearm sharply across her arm, breaking her contact with his face, then he scrambled to catch her wrist. Damn it, he could feel fine bones and slenderness, but there was a wild strength in Alicia that he'd never dealt with before. He caught her left hand, but her right hand landed a blow to his chest that almost knocked the air out of his lungs.

Twisting, he finally got the other hand, and at the same time, he managed to get his legs tangled with hers effectively enough to hold them down. Using the weight of his body to pin her under him on the bed he managed to catch both wrists in his left hand, jerked them over her head onto the bed, and drew his other hand back in a fist. Every instinct of survival in him was to knock her out, to stop the frantic struggling, but with his hand closed into a fist and raised to strike, he stopped dead.

His rapid breathing echoed in the room, almost in sync with hers. Her eyes were wide and bright with a mixture of anger and fear. Her skin was flushed with high color, and her breasts, under a heavy white sweater, rose and fell rapidly. Both her hands, caught by his, were in fists, and she fought against his restraint. She wasn't cringing from him, even though he had total control now, and all he had to do was strike her to get it over with.

"You're crazy...!" she choked. "I... I..." She took a deep, shuddering breath and gasped, "Get off me."

He wasn't about to move, keeping his hand high, ready to strike if he had to. "How much are you getting paid?" he demanded. Someway, breaking it down into terms of money for services rendered made it easier for him to deal with right now. "How much, damn it?"

She shook her head sharply from side to side, her hair tangling around his arm. "You're crazy. Just let me go. I'll leave. I'll get out of here right now." She tried to pull her hands free of his and sit up, but Steven only tightened his hold. She sank back. "Please, just let me go."

It was hard to look into those green eyes, to see the edge of vulnerability there and not just move back. He sucked in air, forcing himself to regain his control, but with her under him, he was having a hell of a time calming down. "I'll let you go when you tell me the truth."

Alicia stared up at Buck over her and knew she was living her worst nightmare. She was totally at his mercy and he was stark-raving mad. His black hair swung forward, his blue eyes narrowed ominously, and the bulky coat he had on only emphasized his size. She had never been one to feel helpless. She'd learned early on how to take care of herself, but with Buck, she knew she was in way over her head. And the worst thing was she didn't even know *what* she'd gotten into. The gun, his anger, his isolation—none of it added up to anything she could understand.

If she could just free her hands...but she couldn't. Her only hope was to try and talk to him. "All right, just tell me what you want."

He inhaled and exhaled harshly, then said, "I want answers."

She closed her eyes to shut out the sight of him over her, but opened them immediately. She hadn't realized until then how a world of darkness made every other sensation come to life. She didn't need to feel his weight on her, the hard strength of his body imprisoning hers or the heat of his breath on her face. She met his intense gaze. "What are the questions?"

"Who are you?"

He really was crazy. But the look in his eyes wasn't insanity. It was pure, raw anger. "You know who I am."

His grip on her wrists tightened more, hovering just this side of real pain. "Who...are...you?" he ground out, his jaw clenched.

"Alicia Sullivan," she said quickly. "I...I've got my ID in my wallet. It's—"

"He sent you, didn't he?"

"Who?"

"Shaw."

"I don't understand any of this. I thought you were a good Samaritan, and all the time, you...you were just..."

"*You* were just biding your time," he managed. "But I've got bad news for you. Shaw's not going to get his way this time."

"Shaw? His way? It's you who hit me and landed on top of me and won't get off."

"You had the gun."

She blinked. "What?"

"You had the gun."

She closed her eyes for a moment, then looked back up at Buck. "*Your* gun. I found it under the mattress when I was making the bed. It's not mine. I thought it was yours."

He exposed a degree of uncertainty in his expression for just a moment, then it was gone. "I saw you with it."

Stay calm. Just stay calm, she told herself. *You've been in tighter fixes than this. Just get out of it and run.* "I found it. I looked at it. I was putting it back. And now I want to get up and leave. I'll let you have your privacy. Just let me get out of here."

"So you can go back to Shaw and tell him where I am, what I'm going to do?"

"I don't know anyone called Shaw, and I'm not about to tell anyone where you are . . . or what you're doing."

She could feel his hold on her falter, and she almost used that moment to escape. But something in her told her that she had to ease out of this. In a one-on-one fight with Buck, she didn't stand a prayer of a chance. He kept silent, just looking at her as if he was trying to decide if he believed her or not.

"I swear I was just looking at the gun," she said quickly. "I hate guns. I always have. You can have the gun if you want it. I don't want it. I don't even know how to work one. I wouldn't work one. I don't think I could even if I had lessons."

"Shoot."

"What?"

"It's not 'work,' it's 'shoot,'" he muttered and rolled off to one side, giving her her freedom in a heartbeat.

She lay very still for a moment, then drew her hands in front of her face. Red bands circled her wrists, and she knew they'd bruise soon. "I don't know what's going on, but I'm out of here."

She sat up and looked at Buck. He was on his back, his hair spread on the sheets, his gaze on a spot on the ceiling over him. "You can't leave," he murmured without looking at her.

She spotted the gun across the room at the base of the half wall that separated the bedroom area from the living area. For a second she thought about getting it, then knew how stupid that would be. She'd been telling the truth. She couldn't shoot anyone, not even this madman. "I sure can leave," she said, getting to her feet.

Buck didn't move, but his eyes met hers. "Go ahead and try, but it won't do you any good. You'll end up dying out there this time."

She turned and looked at the door that was still ajar. Even from here she could see the snow that had tumbled in on the hardwood floor. She crossed to the door and pulled it back. Snow had completely obliterated the shape of the porch, the drifts so deep that the windows were partially covered. She could see where Buck had trudged through it, heading toward the garage and shed, but any real path was gone. The snow looked soft and blindly white, and probably three feet deep.

"Where's Pax?" she asked, aware the dog wasn't anywhere to be seen.

"I don't know."

Alicia turned and saw Buck was standing. He stripped off his jacket, dropped it over the back of the couch and went for the gun. He picked it up, and as he straightened, he pushed it into the waistband at the back of his jeans as if he'd done it all his life. And maybe he had, for all she knew.

"Wasn't Pax with you?"

Buck crossed to her, and stopped with not more than two feet separating them. "He was, but he headed out toward the slide area when I came back."

"Slide area?"

"The avalanche was just down the way. It buried a whole section of trees, but no houses." He looked past her, out the door. "It felt like it was coming right down on us."

The chill at her back made her tremble. "I've never felt anything like that, except for an earthquake." She reached to swing the door shut, then went past Buck to the couch. "I guess I can't walk to the car, can I?"

"You can if you want to try, but what are you going to do when you get there? You said it was partly buried and it's out of gas."

"Don't you have gas in the garage?"

"I don't know. If there's gas out there, it wouldn't be more than a gallon."

It amazed her that they were talking so civilly, when moments ago they'd been fighting as if their lives depended on it. Now Buck was calm, almost emotionless, and Alicia watched him carefully, wondering if he could explode again without warning. She tucked her feet under her. "What about Pax?"

"What about him?"

"Why didn't you bring him back with you?"

Buck crossed to the fireplace and crouched down in front of the hearth to start laying logs on the grate. "I can't make him do anything," he said. "You, better than anyone else, should know that."

Alicia stared at the gun in his waistband and she swallowed hard. Something in her didn't believe that Buck really wanted to hurt her, but she couldn't forget his hand clenched in a fist over her. Something was wrong, horribly wrong. And she literally couldn't get away unless she wanted to freeze to death in the snow.

"Buck?"

He reached for a match from a small container on the hearth and spoke without turning as he struck the match on the stones. "What?"

"What's the gun for?"

His hand stilled, and the match almost burned down to his thumb and forefinger before he finally shook it out. "Protection," he said at last as he lit another match and tossed it into the fireplace.

"Protection from what?"

He didn't respond until he turned and sat on the hearth. As he looked at Alicia, he tucked his hair behind his ears, emphasizing his high cheekbones and exotic eyes. Unreadable eyes. "Protection. Period."

She didn't back down. "Who's Shaw?"

"Who's Alicia Sullivan?" he countered.

She had tried so hard to change in the past year that she truly didn't know just who she was anymore. She wasn't about to discuss that with this man. "I asked you first."

He took his time tugging off his boots and setting them on the hearth before he answered her. "I used to work for Shaw."

"Why would he send *me* here?"

She could see the tension growing in Buck. His voice was more and more remote, yet she had the distinct feeling his emotions were in full play. He just hid them well. "You tell me."

"Boy, I hate that," she said.

"Hate what?"

"I hate games, and that's what you're doing. You would have killed me a few minutes ago, and now you're sitting there with a gun stuck in the back of your pants answering my questions with your own oblique questions."

His mouth thinned, but his voice stayed controlled. "I'm trying to act civilized."

"I think that might be too much to hope for," she muttered before she thought.

"And it's too much to hope that you'll hold your tongue, isn't it?"

She stood, then knew she had no place to go. There was no privacy in this cabin and no hope of going anywhere outside. "At least I didn't say it was sad."

"But I bet you thought it."

She rubbed at her right wrist. "Oh, now you can read my mind?"

"Don't I wish," he said as he stood and came across to face her. Before she knew what he was going to do, he reached out and caught her hands with his. Her flinch was instinctive and instant. But this time he wasn't trying to control her.

He drew her hands toward him, then looked down at her wrists. "My God, I didn't know I did that to you."

She glanced down at her hands caught in his, and her first reaction was how dark his skin looked against hers, how strong his fingers were. Then she saw the bruises she'd known would come. Pale bracelets that showed where he'd held her so tightly.

"Why did you do it?" she asked, looking up to meet the blue intensity of his gaze. "And don't tell me something about this Shaw. I don't know anyone called Shaw and I couldn't care less if you worked for him. I want to know why you tackled me like that."

He drew back, releasing her hands. "You don't let go, do you?"

"A bad trait, sort of like talking to myself. Why did you tackle me?"

"I misunderstood what was going on."

"Misunderstood what?"

"You with a gun."

"It was *your* gun."

"I didn't know that when I came in." He combed his fingers through his hair. "All I saw was the gun. I overreacted."

"You sure did. Are you going to tell me why?"

"Probably not. I doubt that you'd understand even if I did."

"You could try."

He reached to touch her cheek, and when she flinched, he cupped her chin with warmth and strength. "Don't do that."

"What?"

"I know I've given you plenty of reason, but don't be afraid of me."

She absorbed his touch and knew she was afraid, but not of any harm she thought he could do to her. It wasn't the fear of harm that made her heart race or her skin flush. She didn't dare move at all. "I'm just confused," she admitted.

"You aren't the only one," he whispered, then lowered his head and touched his lips to hers.

Alicia had no preparation for the contact and no defense against the emotions that raged through her the instant his warmth touched her lips. Time stopped, and the world ground to a halt. The pressure was light and tentative, yet it riveted Alicia, and before he drew back, she had time for one clear thought. No one had ever touched her like this before in her life. No one.

Her basic instinct was to move closer, to open her mouth to his, to hold on to him for dear life, but before she could do anything, Buck drew back. His blue eyes burned into hers, and she could see the way his nostrils flared with each rapid breath he took.

When his gaze dropped to her parted lips, she was certain he was going to kiss her again. And it terrified her when she realized that was exactly what she wanted him to do. And she'd thought he was mad? *She* was crazy. When he gently stroked her cheek with the tips of his fingers, she trembled.

"I'm sorry," he said in a low, vaguely hoarse voice.

She didn't know if he was apologizing for the attack on her or the kiss. And she wasn't about to ask. Both contacts had unnerved her. She turned her head away from his touch and sank down on the couch.

She sensed Buck moving, then he was sitting in the chair to the right of the couch. When she chanced a look at him, he was sitting low, his long legs stretched out in front of him, and he stared at the fire.

"You aren't going to tell me what's happening, are you?" she said.

He rested his head on the back of the chair and closed his eyes. "No. I can't." And he effectively shut her out.

Alicia watched Buck, the way his hair fell back from his face, exposing the line of his jaw and throat. And she touched her lips, as if she could capture the feeling that had been there moments before. But she couldn't. It was gone, as if it had never been. Yet its effects were still making her heart beat faster and her stomach knot.

No man had kissed her like that before. No Mick Terrine had ever made her think of heat and passion with only the fleeting contact of his mouth. No one. Not even Jon. Yet just looking at Buck, she felt a restlessness that she couldn't define, a need for something more.

What I need, she told herself, *is to get to Jon and to sanity.* She knew all too well what insanity could cost. She'd seen the price in her life too many times. She reached for the phone, but before she could put it to her ear, Buck said, "It's still dead. The lines outside are all up, but there's no connection."

She looked at him, his eyes still closed, and she pushed back into the corner of the couch. "How long do you think it will be before they fix the lines?"

"No idea."

"What about Pax?"

"What about the animal?"

"Can't you go and find him?"

"Go where?"

"Wherever he went. You just can't leave him out there. He could be lost, and it's freezing. You know how cold it is out there."

He opened his eyes and cast her a slanting look that showed disbelief. "Oh, no. Forget it. I'm not going out in that cold to look for a dog who's too dumb to know where he should be."

"You don't have to." She stood and looked around for her boots, then spotted them by the bed and went to get them. "I'll go and look. You stay here." She sat on the bed and pushed her feet into them.

When she stood, Buck was on his feet, too. "You aren't going out there on some damned rescue mission."

She ignored the dampness still inside her boots. "I'll just walk around by the cabin and call for him."

"Wasn't one freezing near-death experience enough for you?"

She spotted her jacket on the rack by the door and walked past Buck to get it. "I won't freeze to death. It's not snowing now, and I can see the cabin." She shrugged into her jacket. "I'll just go out and call for him."

Buck got to the door at the same time as she gripped the doorknob. His hand closed over hers and held to it tightly, preventing her from opening the door. "I said you aren't going out there."

She looked at his hand over hers, then made herself look up into his eyes. "What are you going to do, pull the gun on me and shoot me?"

She saw the nerve twitch in his jaw as he stared at her hard. Then he broke his contact with her. He turned and went to the couch to grab his coat. Without looking at her, he slipped it on, then got his boots and pushed them on. "I'm coming with you."

If truth be told, she wasn't easy about going outside by herself, but she wouldn't admit that to Buck. "If you want to, but let's get going." She opened the door, pushed her hands into her pockets and stepped out onto the porch.

Even though she tucked her chin into her collar, the cold air stung her cheeks before she managed to get to the edge of the porch. She heard the door close, then Buck brushed past her and stopped by the porch post nearest the buried steps.

"Where did you see Pax last?" Alicia asked.

Buck pointed to the south. "That way, back closer to the mountain." He stepped off the porch and sank up to his midcalf in the snow. As he started off to the south, he spoke over his shoulder to Alicia. "Try to stay in my footprints. It'll make it easier for you."

She did what he said, stepping down into the holes he left with each step. Yet before they even got to the corner of the cabin, her feet felt like lead. But when Buck kept going, she made herself keep up with him.

As they cleared the cabin, Buck turned to the left and Alicia followed him. She looked up and saw the mountains, towering behemoths cutting into the sky. And as they moved away from the cabin, she could see the first signs of the avalanche. Monstrous clumps of snow lay on the slope, looking as if they had literally broken off the mountain and tumbled to the ground.

She stopped and cupped her hands to her mouth. "Pax! Pax!" Only her voice echoed back to her.

Buck never stopped, and Alicia hurried after him, scanning the whiteness for any sign of the dog. "Damn it, he has to be here somewhere. There isn't any place for him to go." She hated the feeling of loss she felt at

SILHOUETTE®

N IMPORTANT MESSAGE
ROM THE EDITORS OF
LHOUETTE®

ar Reader,

cause you've chosen to read one of our
e romance novels, we'd like to say
hank you"! And, as a **special** way to
ank you, we've selected <u>four more</u> of the
oks you love so well, **and** a Victorian
cture Frame to send you absolutely *FREE!*

ease enjoy them with our compliments...

*Leslie
Wager*

Senior Editor,
Silhouette Intimate Moments

S. And because we value our
stomers, we've attached something
xtra inside ...

HOW TO VALIDATE
YOUR
EDITOR'S FREE GIFT
"THANK YOU"

1. Peel off gift seal from front cover. Place it in space provided at right. This automatically entitles you to receive four free books and a lovely pewter-finish Victorian picture frame.

2. Send back this card and you'll get brand-new Silhouette Intimate Moments® novels. These books have a cover price of $3.39 each, but they are yours to keep absolutely free.

3. There's no catch. You're under no obligation to buy anything. We charge nothing–ZERO–for your first shipment. And you don't have to make any minimum number of purchases–not even one!

4. The fact is thousands of readers enjoy receiving books by mail from the Silhouette Reader Service™ months before they're available in stores. They like the convenience of home delivery and they love our discount prices!

5. We hope that after receiving your free books you'll want to remain a subscriber. But the choice is yours–to continue or cancel, anytime at all! So why not take us up on our invitation, with no risk of any kind. You'll be glad you did!

6. Don't forget to detach your FREE BOOKMARK. And remember…just for validating your Editor's Free Gift Offer we'll send you FIVE MORE gifts, *ABSOLUTELY FREE!*

YOURS FREE!
*This lovely Victorian pewter-finish miniature is perfect for displaying a treasured photograph–and it's yours **absolutely free**–when you accept our no-risk offer!*

THE EDITOR'S "THANK YOU" FREE GIFTS INCLUDE:

▶ Four BRAND-NEW romance novels
▶ A pewter-finish Victorian picture frame

THE SILHOUETTE READER SERVICE™: HERE'S HOW IT WORKS

Accepting free books puts you under no obligation to buy anything. You may keep the books and gift and return the shipping statement marked "cancel." If you do not cancel, about a month later we will send you 6 additional novels, and bill you just $2.71 each plus 25¢ delivery and applicable sales tax if any*. That's the complete price, and—compared to the cover price of $3.39 each—quite a bargain! You may cancel at any time, but if you choose to continue, every month we'll send you 6 more books, which you may either purchase at the discount price . . . or return at our expense and cancel your subscription.

* Terms and prices subject to change without notice. Sales tax applicable in N.Y.

If offer card is missing write to: Silhouette Reader Service, 3010 Walden Ave., P.O. Box 1867, Buffalo, NY 14269-1867

BUSINESS REPLY MAIL
FIRST CLASS MAIL   PERMIT NO. 717   BUFFALO, NY

POSTAGE WILL BE PAID BY ADDRESSEE

SILHOUETTE READER SERVICE
3010 WALDEN AVE
PO BOX 1867
BUFFALO NY 14240-9952

NO POSTAGE
NECESSARY
IF MAILED
IN THE
UNITED STATES

the idea the dog was gone. "He has to be here somewhere."

Buck stopped and turned back to Alicia. "Were you talking to me?"

"Nothing, I was just talking to myself," she said and kept walking.

Then they crested a low hill and she saw the avalanche itself. She could see a gaping crater on the side of the mountain, then a long slide area that went to the bottom and ended in a tremendous mound of snow. When she saw the splotches of green breaking the pure white, she realized they were the tops of trees that had been buried under tons of the slide. No wonder the cabin had trembled and the air had been filled with the rumblings of the fall.

Sampson sat alone in his office in Washington, D.C., his chair turned so he could look down Pennsylvania Avenue. A layer of fresh snow that had fallen during the night made the city look beautiful. It hid all the ugly things that went on so close to the nation's capital.

He rocked back in his chair and ran his hand over his almost nonexistent hair. "Shorn like Sampson," someone had said, and the code name Sampson had stuck when he dealt in covert actions and couldn't use his real name, Larry Getz. He knew this was the last time he could use the code name, but right now, a code name was the least of his worries.

He was cut off from Rider. He wondered if he should send out someone to get to the man any way they could. With the phones down, it made him nervous not to have contact. Contact meant control, and he had lost control when nature decided to dump three feet of snow on the Rockies.

But the snow that blocked him would also block any attempt Shaw might make. And before Shaw could do anything, he had to figure out where Rider was hidden and track him down. Nervousness went with the territory, and Sampson always thought in worst-case scenarios. This case wasn't any different. Prepare for the worst and never be surprised.

He swivelled around when someone knocked on his door, and he pressed both hands to the coolness of the desk. "Come in," he called out.

Jaye Delancy, one of the rookie agents working with him, hurried into the office. "Sir, this just came in over the restricted line," he said as he handed him a fax. "It's got your code number on it."

Sampson read the coded message and realized the worst-case scenario was close to becoming reality. "Get Russell in here right now," he snapped.

"Yes, sir," Delancy said and hurried out, closing the door behind him.

Sampson looked back down at the paper, and automatically translated it. *"Shaw's got Sobba working for him. S. left Seattle and dropped out of sight. Former security clearance covered the sites. Possible goal—Denver."*

Lewis Sobba, a.k.a. Jaimie L., was loose, and Shaw had him. If anyone could find Rider, Sobba could. And if anyone would kill Rider without blinking, Sobba would. Sampson had no doubt he was on his way to Colorado. "So am I," he muttered as he fed the paper into the shredder.

* * *

Buck stayed ahead of Alicia, not looking back. He didn't want to see her right now, not the brilliant hair or the green eyes or anything that had driven him to kiss her before. Mistake number one million in his life. That's the last thing he needed, to taste her and not be able to get that essence out of his mind.

He wasn't used to not being able to make a decision. Was she from Shaw or wasn't she? The longer she was here, the more he doubted it, yet something in him, that basic instinct of survival, wouldn't let him forget the possibility. It had been his gun this time, but the next time...

"Pax! Pax!" she called from behind him, cutting into his thoughts.

He stopped and scanned the avalanche area ahead. The snow from the storm and the avalanche obliterated everything ahead, and blocked any chance they had of going much farther. But he didn't want to go back. Not back to the cabin and being closed in with Alicia again.

She came to his side and spoke to him. "Where do you think he would have gone?"

"Back where he came from," he said, never taking his eyes off the land in front of him.

"Don't you have any idea where he belongs?"

"No."

"Did you ask your neighbors?"

"I've never met my neighbors." He glanced at her and wished he hadn't. The brilliance he had known would be there was breathtaking. Damn it all. He felt as if he were at the breaking point. Nothing was right. Nothing was the way it should have been. Certainly not the feelings this woman could stir up in him with one glance, or if she got any closer to him than fifty feet.

He turned abruptly to head back. "We can't go any farther," he said, retracing his own steps.

Without a word, she followed him, and he kept his eyes down. From time to time he saw her footprints over his in the snow, or he saw places where she'd swung her hands across the top crust of the snow. She'd stopped at one point—the half circles she'd made in the snow were deeper and more pronounced.

"Pax!" The sound of her voice startled him as they neared the cabin, and the way it echoed off the land all around seemed to vibrate in him. Then he realized how exposed he was out here, how exposed they both were, something he hadn't even thought about until now. A major slip, a potentially deadly slip. As long as Alicia was even at the cabin, she could be in danger because of him.

He was about to turn and tell her to stop calling and to get back into the house, when he caught a sharp movement by the cabin.

Chapter 8

Steven tensed, but before his hand could go for the gun still tucked in his waistband, the dog cleared the side of the building.

Using the crude path Steven and Alicia had made earlier, the animal moved toward them with an easy lope that annoyed Steven. Almost as much as the way his heart was hammering annoyed him.

He heard Alicia behind him say, "Good dog, Pax. I knew you wouldn't leave just like that."

Her voice got closer to Steven at about the same rate as the dog did. When she brushed against his arm, the dog was there, and without sparing Steven a glance, he launched himself at Alicia.

Steven turned as Alicia put out her hands, and the dog landed against her with his two front paws on her chest, sending her sprawling backward. Dog and woman tangled together and almost disappeared into the whiteness of the snow.

Steven wondered if it was his life's avocation to be rescuing this woman from all manner of things—blizzards, fainting, and now a dog. But before he could reach for the animal to pull him off Alicia, he heard laughter.

He moved closer, stood over the two of them, and he saw Alicia lying in the snow with the dog on top of her. Her arms were around the animal's neck and he was nuzzling her hair. As the sound of her laughter rang in the frigid air, Steven felt more like an outsider than he ever had before. There had been no feelings like this, not even when he'd been a boy, or when he'd been on the road, or even when he knew he had to leave Steven Rider behind.

When Alicia looked past the dog and up at Steven, he saw pure pleasure in her eyes. "See. He didn't run away," she said.

Steven narrowed his eyes in an attempt to block the vision of her smiling up at him from the snow. "Are you going to lie in the snow until you freeze to death?" he muttered.

"I'm not going to freeze," she said as she let her arms fall to her sides while the dog licked her face. "Didn't you ever play in the snow when you were a little kid?"

Steven remembered hiding in the snow, staying out of the house to be well out of the way when his father went on one of his drunken rampages. Play? He couldn't remember doing that in the snow. "I don't even remember when I was a little kid," he lied.

She sat up, holding the dog off with one hand, and cocked her head to one side as she studied Steven. "No snowmen? No snowballs? No snow forts? No snow angels?"

He shook his head, hunching his shoulders against the wind as it picked up. "No." He frowned at her. "And it's cold out here."

The dog stood by Alicia and looked up at Steven.

"I haven't thought about snow angels in a while," Alicia said. In the next breath, she fell back and began to move her arms up and down, making arches in the snow, and moving her legs back and forth. Just when he thought she'd taken complete leave of her senses, she stopped and carefully got up.

Snow clung to her hair and the back of her clothes, and she came to stand by Steven, then turned and pointed down at the impression she'd left in the snow. "Voilà, a snow angel."

Angel? Maybe if he blurred his eyes and looked at it from a strange angle. "If you say so," he muttered. "We need to get inside. I—"

Alicia turned and hurried toward the cabin. For a moment he thought she was obeying him without an argument, then he realized she wasn't going to the porch. She made her way to the side wall where the protection of the structure had made the snow less deep.

"It looks better in fresh snow," she called to him, and turning around to face him, she held out her arms and fell back into snow under the small bathroom window. As she duplicated her actions of moments ago, Steven wished he could get past the beauty of the smile of enjoyment on her face.

God, he envied her. And he envied Jon, who'd have this woman with him for the rest of his life. Maybe there really was happiness in this life for some people.

She got to her feet, careful not to disturb what she'd done, then turned and looked down at the image she'd made in the snow. "Now, *that's* a snow angel for the world to see."

The world. He could feel uneasiness prickling at the back of his neck, and he scanned the area. Anyone could see them out here. Not a thing moved, but he couldn't get past the feeling of being totally exposed. And when Alicia touched his arm, his uneasiness increased. Physical exposure to danger was one thing, but he could tell there was an emotional exposure to danger with this woman that could be just as devastating.

"What do you think?" she asked, her hand resting on his arm.

"It's fine," he said, moving his gaze to the impression in the snow and away from Alicia. He shrugged sharply, using it as cover to move away from her touch. "Too bad you can't make money doing it."

She laughed at that, and the sound only disturbed him more. "You sound just like Harry used to. He taught me how to make snow angels and how to do a lot of things. And he used to say that it was too bad he knew so much about things that no one would pay a penny for him to do."

"Smart man," Steven murmured, looking back at Alicia. "But how did he teach you about snow in L.A.?" he asked, keeping his body between her and the road.

"Harry used to take us up to the mountains every year after the first big snow, you know, when the roads were cleared and the skies were blue. Not like the storm last night. Harry used to say that places that snowed were nice places to visit, but not to live."

The dog pushed himself between Steven and Alicia, and she dropped her hand to touch the animal's head while she stared at the snow angel. Steven couldn't take his eyes off Alicia, off the delicate sweep of her jaw, her hair glistening with the dampness of melting snow and the way she nibbled on her bottom lip as she studied what she'd done.

"I always wanted to go to Montana," she said without warning. "I hear it snows there like there's no tomorrow. Or maybe Connecticut. I've seen pictures that make it look like a Norman Rockwell painting."

"You want to live there?"

"No, just to visit. I like California. I wouldn't want to live any other place."

"Even with the earthquakes?"

"I'd take them any day over avalanches."

"Personally, I'd just as soon leave both of them. And if you want to travel, that shouldn't be a problem, since you're a travel agent."

"I'm not an agent, just a helper. I need more training to be an agent." She looked up at him. "I've traveled a lot, but I always seemed to go to warm places... until now. You know something else that Harry taught me?"

He wanted to say that Harry couldn't have possibly taught her how to look this good when she was wet from snow and her nose was red from the cold. "What's that?" he asked.

"How to make the perfect snowball," she said as she reached down and grabbed a handful of snow. Without taking her eyes off Steven, she formed the snow in her slender hands, she shaped it into a ball, then held it up to show him. "Perfect, huh?" One eyebrow raised in a questioning arch.

"It looks like any snowball."

"But it's not. It's perfect," she said.

"A snowball's a snowball, and we have to get inside."

"You're wrong," she said. She turned and pointed to one of the trees that was about twenty feet from the cabin. "If a snowball's perfect, you can hit a target without the snowball falling apart in midair on the way."

"That's the test of a perfect snowball?"

"That's what Harry used to say."

"And if Harry said it, it has to be so?"

She nodded, then turned sideways, drew her hand with the snowball back over her shoulder behind her ear and threw it. Steven watched the snowball arch through the air, the sunlight glinting off the ice crystals in it. With a soft thud, it struck near the top of the tree and loosened a clump of snow that fell to the ground with a whoosh.

Alicia turned to him, a smile lighting up her face. "See? Perfect." She rubbed her hands briskly on her jacket, then reached for more snow. "Now, if you're going to be throwing it at someone, you don't make it that way."

She patted at the snow in her hands. "You leave some air in it so it's softer... unless you want to hurt someone." She crinkled up her nose. "Snow stings something horrible if you pack it too tightly. My sister used to make snowballs that felt like rocks, and that's not fair.'' She held up the new snowball. ''Another perfect snowball.''

He shrugged. ''I hate to say it, but it looks like the other one.'' The growing wind lifted his hair. The chill air was beginning to feel raw, and he couldn't stand out here in the open debating this woman about snowballs. ''It's time to go back inside, Alicia.''

He started off, but Alicia didn't move. ''It's not like the other one,'' she called after him.

''Couldn't prove it by me,'' he murmured and kept going.

As he got near the porch, the dog bounded past him and headed for the door. But before he could step up on the porch himself, he felt a thud between his shoulder blades. It jarred him even though the impact was little more than a bump, and he spun around, adrenalin pumping through him.

But there was no danger behind him, just Alicia standing in calf-deep snow, her head tipped to one side, her hands on her hips. ''See, it didn't hurt, did it? I told you it wasn't like the other one.''

She looked like a brilliant gem in the whiteness all around, a brilliant gem who was reaching for more snow. Steven started back toward her, but was no more than halfway there when he saw the next snowball forming in her hands. Before he could do more than lift his hand, another snowball hit him in the chest.

''Stop it,'' he called out to Alicia.

''Didn't hurt, either, did it?'' she returned as she scooped up more snow. ''I told you it wouldn't. Plain snow doesn't hurt, either.''

"Don't you dare—!" His words were cut off when she tossed the handful of snow at him. Icy moisture went in his eyes and his mouth and snuck under his collar. He swiped at his face and saw Alicia back-pedaling awkwardly in the snow. Her eyes glowed with humor, her lips curved with a mischievous smile, and she had more snow in her hands. Her breath curled into the cold air as she called out, "You should have ducked."

He reached to his side and scooped up a handful of snow. Moving as quickly as he could after her, he made a ball, then watched her eyes grow wide when he raised his hand. She turned with a burst of laughter as he threw it, and it caught her right between her shoulder blades.

"You should have ducked," he said as he closed the distance between them.

Alicia's laughter was everywhere and as Steven reached her, she turned with another snowball in her hands. Before she could throw it, he had her by her shoulders. His momentum carried them both back into the snow. And as they tumbled into the drift, Alicia's laughter rang in his ears, and her being seemed tangled with his.

Cold, wet snow pushed up his sleeves and soaked through his jeans, but as he caught himself over Alicia, his hands pressed in the snow on either side of her flame-colored hair, he felt a heat that defied the world all around him. Her eyes, the flush to her cheeks, her parted lips, all built a fire in Steven that threatened to consume him.

"Alicia." He breathed her name, almost tasting it on his tongue.

The world could go to hell for all he cared at that moment, and it probably would, but he didn't move. He watched the pattern of her breath curling in the air, mingling with his in the cold air. And he felt his whole being tighten.

"That was a pretty poor excuse for a snowball," Alicia said, her voice soft and suddenly breathless.

"It didn't hurt?"

"Was it supposed to?"

There was no way he'd ever want to hurt this woman. "No, it wasn't supposed to," he said, his mind racing with the idea that she was a woman to cherish and to love. "Definitely not supposed to hurt."

"Then it was perfect," she breathed.

Perfection was right here with him, under him, lying in the snow with him. And Steven knew it as surely as he knew he had no right to do what he was going to at this moment. He looked into her green eyes, into the laughter and softness, and lowered his head.

Alicia looked up at Buck, and everything changed. As he moved closer to her, as his hair brushed her face, she knew what was going to happen. And she realized in that moment that she'd wanted it to happen since he'd kissed her in the cabin. A stranger who could turn her bones to water and block out reality, who made her want things she'd never thought she'd want before.

When his lips touched hers, she held her breath. Then his mouth covered hers, but this time it wasn't fleeting and elusive. This time she felt the heat and strength, the way his hair tickled her skin, the brush of the beginnings of a beard against her face. And the most natural thing in the world right then was to wrap her arms around his neck, to pull him even closer until the snow and cold were gone.

Alicia tasted and relished him, the feel of his tongue softly parting her lips, his invasion, the way he ran his tongue over her teeth. The insanity of the moment felt like sanity, and her need for more from him seemed as right as the need to breathe air. She welcomed the intimacy, arching toward him, her fingers sinking in his thick hair. And the kiss deepened, the need transforming into a fiery desire that she'd never felt before.

With the bulky jackets, it was impossible for Alicia to touch Buck the way she wanted to. She wanted skin against skin, to run her hands over his chest, to feel the muscles, to taste the heat and maleness of him. Every impulse in her wanted to be with Buck. Every atom of her being wanted more, to know him, to share herself with him.

Frantically, she tugged at his jacket, parting the zipper until she worked her hands under the leather and against his shirt. She could feel heat and the thudding of his heart. And when he tasted her throat and that sensitive spot under her ear, she trembled with need.

Then Buck drew back, his face inches from hers, his breath curling into the coldness all around. And she could see the same needs in him that were coming to life in her. She could feel the strength of that need like a living thing in her. A stranger, but one she felt as if she must have bonded with in another life. There was a joining that went beyond the physical, and a sense of finding a part of herself that she'd never known she'd lost.

He was a man she could easily love, if she let herself. A man who could make her dream dreams and weave fantasies. A dangerous man. A man with secrets. And the truth hit her hard. Impulsiveness was her worst enemy. It could destroy her, and it probably would if she let herself act on it. She looked up at Buck, and she realized how single-mindedly she wanted this man.

It was the same pattern as she followed with Mick Terrine, only this time instead of a dangerous criminal, it was an overwhelmingly fascinating Buck.... She didn't even know his last name. No, she couldn't leap before looking again. She couldn't risk everything. She couldn't lose her new life, her sanity, for a few moments of pleasure.

When Alicia closed her eyes, Steven knew he was so far over the edge that if he didn't pull himself back, he'd take her. His need for her was achingly real, and he knew he had no right to even feel it. He had no right to want this woman, to want to make love with her and to wake with her by him in the morning. He had no rights at all.

There was no place in his life for her, because he simply didn't have a life. As he looked at her, he knew that if he ever stepped over the line with her, he wouldn't be able to just walk away. No way in hell. And they'd both pay for it, maybe with their lives.

She opened her eyes, and when he met her gaze, he felt as if he had been robbed of the power to leave. A green-eyed witch who cast a spell, he thought, a witch who could almost make him think life could be different. But when he heard the dog barking from near the house, it gave him the impetus to back off.

In one movement, he was on his feet, looking in the direction of the dog. The wind had picked up, rustling the trees and tugging at the snow-laden branches. But beyond the sounds of the dog and the wind, he heard something else. He stood very still, scanning the area, but he couldn't see anything. Then he heard the noise again, the sound of a motor off in the distance.

He turned to Alicia who had scrambled to her feet and was brushing at the snow that clung to her clothes. Even when he spoke, she wouldn't look at him. "I think the plows are out."

She looked toward the road, listened, then went past Steven to head for the cabin. "Good," she muttered. "Then I can get out of here."

Steven couldn't move. *And anyone else can get* in *here*. He let her go, waiting until she was on the porch and going into the cabin with the dog at her heels. He took time to calm down, to at least get his body back to normal before he followed her into the cabin. When he stepped inside, Alicia had discarded her coat and boots, and was standing in the middle of the living area. She glanced at him as he closed the door behind him, but she didn't quite make eye contact.

"Would you have another shirt I could borrow while my pants dry? They're . . . damp from the snow."

He moved past her, tossing his coat onto the couch as he went, and he tugged open the top drawer of his dresser. He took out a shirt and turned to toss it on the bed. "There's a shirt," he said without looking at her, and he went toward the kitchen. "I'll make some food."

Alicia didn't move until Buck was in the kitchen. Then she moved to the bed, picked up the shirt and kept going to the bathroom. Once in the small room, she closed the door, then leaned back against it, hugging the shirt to her breasts.

"Damn it all, Alicia, get a grip," she muttered to herself. "This isn't some game. You don't even know anything about the man, yet you're rolling around in the snow with him as if you're some teenager with an excess of hormones."

She moved away from the door and dropped the shirt on the sink. She stripped off the damp corduroy pants, then tugged her sweater off and reached for the shirt. Once again she felt the cotton of Buck's shirt on her skin, but this time all it did was remind her how the man had felt over her.

She reached for the brush, tugging it through her damp curls, and welcomed the smarting. "Enough is enough," she said to her reflection in the mirror. "Just get out of here when the roads are clear. Think. Don't be a fool. Don't go rushing in where angels fear to tread."

Angels. Snow angels. And she remembered the look on Buck's face the second before she threw the snow at him. Yes, with this man she could rush into things that didn't make any sense at all. She rolled her eyes toward the ceiling and brushed her hair back from her face, the dampness making it curl crazily. "Have some control," she muttered. "He's a man. Just a man."

She dropped her brush on the sink and said to her reflection, "I will not mess up this time."

"Food's ready," Buck called from beyond the door, startling her.

"I'll be right there," she said and quickly buttoned the shirt.

When she stepped back into the bedroom area, Buck was by the bed with his back to her. His bare back. She felt her mouth go dry at the sight and told herself she wasn't some teenager that went weak at the knees because she saw a naked back. But that didn't stop her having to swallow twice to clear her throat as she moved around the bed and passed Buck to go to the kitchen.

Pax was by the fireplace, stretched out absorbing the heat, and he glanced at Alicia as she passed, then settled back down with a grunt. She went into the kitchen, where the small table had been set with bowls of rich-looking soup, crackers and the jar of peanut butter. Buck came up behind her and went to the other side of the table. "Sit and eat," he said as he pulled his chair back.

Alicia sank down on the hard chair and reached for her spoon. What was she supposed to say to this man when she could barely look him in the eye? What do you say to a man who you just kissed, a man you would have probably have made love with if you hadn't come to your senses? She stirred the steaming soup and watched the chunks of vegetables swirl in the broth. "You made this?" she finally asked.

"I opened the can and heated it up."

She made herself look up at him and was inordinately thankful to find him spreading peanut butter on crackers. He casually dipped a cracker in his soup before he popped it in his mouth.

"Peanut butter in soup?" she said without thinking.

Unfortunately that brought his gaze up to meet hers. "It seemed like a good idea when I was six, and it still does," he said as he reached for his spoon.

She avoided his blue gaze by watching her soup as she moved her spoon back and forth in the liquid. "Sort of like banana-and-potato-chip sandwiches?"

"Now, that sounds awful."

"Not any worse than peanut butter in soup."

She looked at him as he tasted the soup, then glanced at her. "What does your fiancé think about your strange tastes?"

She stared at the soup as her spoon stilled. The word *fiancé* sounded wrong in her ears, as discordant as the idea that Buck could have someone, even a wife. She didn't know much about him at all. "He doesn't know."

"That's not good," he said. "Keeping secrets before marriage is a bad omen."

Marriage. Every word he spoke was wrong and jarred Alicia. "That's not exactly a secret," she muttered, and scooped up some soup. "It just never came up in a conversation."

"Does he know you talk to yourself?"

She had just put a mouthful of soup in her mouth and found her throat tightening as she swallowed the rich broth. "That never came up, either," she said without looking at Buck.

"Does he know about snow angels?"

Jon knew the Alicia who was 'normal,' who held a nine-to-five job, who thought before she acted, who was a rational, viable adult. He didn't know the old Alicia. Without warning, her thought completed itself. A stranger who rescued her knew more of the real

Alicia in a day than Jon had come to know in six months.

She sat back in her chair and made herself look at Buck, meet his gaze without flinching. A hard thing to do since the thoughts that ran through her mind were devastating. Jon had never made her feel the way this man had. He had never kissed her like Buck had, and he had never made her wish she could throw caution to the wind and give herself to him.

Los Angeles

Ali walked into Jack's office at the D.A.'s department just before noon. From the doorway, she could see her husband bent over his work, his attention totally focused on the thick files in front of him. With the sleeves of his white shirt rolled up and his red tie gone, he raked his fingers through his sandy blond hair. She shouldn't have come down here today, but she knew he was the only one she could talk to.

"Jack?" she said as she crossed to the front of his desk.

He didn't move for a minute, then he looked up, and the smile when he saw her helped ease the tightness in her. "This is a wonderful surprise," he said. Then the smile changed to a concerned frown. "There isn't anything wrong, is there?"

"No, the baby and I are just fine. It's Alicia."

He sat back in the chair, his smile returning, but touched with a rueful hint now. "What did she do?"

Ali went around the desk and perched on the corner by Jack. "Don't say it like that."

"Like what?"

"Like you always suspected she was a mass murderer and she was just arrested for it."

He touched her hand where it rested on her thigh and stroked the back with the tips of his fingers. "All right. Tell me about Alicia. Just give it to me easy."

"You saw the way she reacted when she thought George Terrine was after her again when she was at the police station?"

"Sure. She was scared. She had every right to be."

"You know when Alicia faces things she can't cope with, she runs and keeps running. She always has."

"I know." He took her hand in his, lacing his fingers with hers. "What's this all about, sweetheart?"

"The phones are still out in Gibson."

"And?"

"I can't get in touch with her."

"If the phones are out, of course you can't get in touch with her."

"I know this sounds strange, but I've got a feeling something's wrong."

"Like what?"

She hated to be this irrational, but she needed to tell Jack. "I don't think she went to Jon's. I don't think she's there at all."

"Is this some psychic twin thing?"

"No. I just know her."

"But, George Terrine is dead. There's no reason for her to take off and run."

"But what if there is?" she asked, her fingers twining in his for support as she voiced her fears.

"What would the reason be?"

"Facing a commitment. Knowing that she's within inches of being what she's always called 'normal.'

Thinking she's being trapped or too close to trusting someone. That scares her, Jack. It always has."

Jack stood and cupped Ali's chin in the warmth of his hand. "You're living in the past, Ali. Alicia's changed."

"Has she?"

He touched his lips to hers, then drew back. "What do you think?"

"Honestly?"

"Honestly."

"I think Alicia is Alicia and she'll never change."

"How about Jon? Doesn't loving someone change everything?"

"It has for me," she murmured, "but Alicia's different. If she was really in love..." Her voice trailed off as she suddenly knew what was bothering her. "I don't think she really loves Jon."

Jack looked surprised. "She told you that?"

"No. She's said the right things about Jon and she loves him, I guess, in a way. But she doesn't *love* him. You know, big-*L* love, instead of the 'he's nice and good-looking and he never yells at me and I think we can get along' kind of love. Not the love she should feel to make a life with him and be happy."

"And what kind of love is that?"

"The 'more than life itself' love," she whispered unsteadily.

"Maybe you're just emotional and missing her. Maybe she loves Jon more than you know." He kissed her again, a gentle caress that almost brought tears to her eyes. "Or maybe you and I are the only two people in the world lucky enough to find a love like that."

She held to Jack, resting her head in the hollow of his shoulder. "Look what we had to go through to find each other."

She felt his laughter rumble against her cheek. "Let's just hope that Alicia doesn't have to sidestep bullets to figure out what she wants."

Chapter 9

Alicia put the phone back in the cradle and sank down on the couch. The fire was roaring, warming the cabin, and outside she could hear the wind growing. She watched Buck cross to the hearth and drop to his haunches by the sleeping dog. Using the poker, he prodded at the fire and made the flames flare and sparks fly upward into the chimney.

"Still dead?" he asked.

"Yes." As Buck shifted to put the poker back, she saw the gun he still had tucked in the back waistband of his jeans. "Buck? Can I ask you something and get a straight answer?"

He dropped the poker back in the holder and turned. As he tucked his hair behind his ears, he looked at Alicia. "It all depends. What do you want to know?"

"The gun. Why do you have one?"

"I thought we'd gone through this before."

"You never explained why it was tucked between the mattress and box spring."

"It was out of the way, but close enough to get to if I needed to." He dropped down in the chair to her right and stretched his long legs out.

"Why would you need it here?"

He studied her for a long moment. "Why wouldn't I?" He laced his fingers together on his stomach and rested his head against the chair back. "Can we change the subject?"

"Sure. What sort of work do you do?"

That brought a deep frown. "A change away from me and what I do."

"That's not fair. I've told you about myself. Tell me about you. What about your family? Have you ever been married? Children, cousins, aunts, uncles? Where were you born, where were you raised, where do you live now?"

He held up one hand palm out to stop her. "Hold on. I hate getting the first degree."

"That's not it. I just wondered about you."

"All right. My mother's dead. My father's off drinking somewhere. I don't have any idea where. He could be dead, for all I know. I'm an only child. I've never been married. I have no children that I know about, and what aunts and uncles I have, I haven't kept in touch with. I was born in Cleveland and raised in Detroit. My last residence was where I worked as a . . . liaison officer."

She stared at him. "A liaison officer?"

He shrugged. "A bodyguard."

A bodyguard. She tucked her legs under her and tugged at the hem of the shirt to cover her thighs. Yes, someway it fit. He was a large man, imposing, almost threatening in appearance. And he sure didn't have a lot of trouble getting the gun away from her.

"That's like a garbage man calling himself a sanitary engineer."

"Close enough," he muttered, no humor in his face. "I guess I've taken out the garbage from time to time."

"And you did it for Shaw?"

His face tightened. "I worked for him."

"As his bodyguard?"

"Bingo. Give the little lady a cigar."

She clasped her hands tightly. "Actually, a cigarette might not be too bad right now."

"You smoke?"

"I used to. I quit about six months ago. But sometimes—"

"You'd kill for a single drag?"

She cocked her head to one side. "Spoken like a reformed smoker."

"It's been five years. Not a puff, but that doesn't mean that I don't have the urge from time to time. Why did you quit?"

She looked down at her hands. "I needed to change things in my life. I'd gone through a crazy period, and I decided that enough was enough. And smoking was part of the past."

"What did you do that was so crazy you had to change everything?"

She almost brushed aside the question with a flip answer, but found she couldn't. Something in her wanted Buck to understand about what she was, what she probably still could be if she didn't watch herself. "I've always done the wrong thing, at the wrong time, with the wrong person. I never meant to be like that, but I was. Harry used to say that I overreacted to being orphaned. That I had this thing in me that always had to be in total control, to not trust anyone, to make sure I wasn't ever involved enough to get hurt.''

She spread her hands palms up. ''Harry wasn't any psychiatrist, but he was right about pretty much everything, but I didn't realize it until last year. I found out then just how much damage I could do to myself and to people I care about.''

Steven watched Alicia and could see the earnestness in her expression tinged with pain. He doubted she could do anything very horrible. ''What happened?''

She dropped her hands to her thighs and closed her eyes for a moment. ''I never told you that my sister and I are identical twins.''

Two Alicias in this world? He doubted the world was ready for that, not on any level.

''And my sister was...she still is...wonderful. She's smart and stable and everything I wish I was. She graduated with honors from high school, and got a good job, and met this great guy and got married last year. They're really happy. She's expecting a child soon.''

''What does this have to do with what you did last year?''

''I don't know how to put this, but . . . did you ever hear of a man called George Terrine?''

''Who the hell hasn't?'' He and Shaw were in the same league, only Terrine was open about who and what he was.

''I sure didn't, not at first.''

He sat forward and rested his elbows on his knees. "You know George Terrine?"

"I knew his son, Mick."

He narrowed his eyes. Was she going to tell him she met the Terrines through Shaw? That what he'd suspected at first was true? "You what?"

"I met Mick Terrine in a casino in Las Vegas. I was dealing blackjack at the time."

He didn't understand any of this. "What's this got to do with—?"

"Let me explain. I'll make this short and not so sweet. I met Mick Terrine. He killed a man, Milt Prince, and he told me about it. The cops found out, and they took me into protective custody until I could testify in front of the grand jury. While I was in custody, Alison, my sister, told me that Lydia, my foster mother, was in the hospital waiting to have open-heart surgery.

"Ali changed places with me so I could go and see Lydia before the operation. We didn't want anyone to know, so the cops and the Terrines thought Ali was me and they tried to kill her. In the end, Ali's husband—at least, he's her husband now, he was my bodyguard then—ended up saving Ali's life, because he thought she was me. Then Mick was killed by this man called Sharp and they let me go."

She spoke so rapidly, words ran into words, but he got the idea. "You didn't have to testify?"

"No, Mick was dead and they thought George Terrine ordered it, if you can believe a father would do that to his son, but Mick was dead, so they told me to go. And Ali and Jack got married, and Lydia came through the operation with flying colors, and I moved to Los Angeles. So you see that I had to change. I couldn't go on like I was. I almost got my sister killed."

Steven felt as if he was being bludgeoned by the flip side of his own life, but he knew that Shaw wouldn't die and his problem wouldn't go away like hers had. "Terrine let it go?"

"Actually, he did, but I didn't believe it until I got the news just before I flew out here that he'd died in his apartment in Las Vegas. Natural causes, they said. So it's really over, and I have to keep my promise."

"What promise?"

"To my sister and to myself, that I'd change. That I'd do things the normal way, that I'd look before I leapt, and I'd never give her any reason to worry again. Then I get stranded in this blizzard and I'm sure that Ali's going crazy because she can't get through to me."

How could she have been in a situation that paralleled his so closely? Was it true? Was it a lie to get his confidence—a misery-loves-company sort of thing? "What's this got to do with not smoking?"

"I told you, I'm changing. I'm doing things the right way. Smoking was definitely stupid. I can control that." She rolled her eyes upward. "That's about the only thing I can control in my life."

"You make it sound as if you're living on the edge."

She almost flinched at the statement, and he wished he hadn't said it. "That's what I've done all my life," she breathed. "That's what I can't do anymore." She blinked, then looked at him. "Why did you quit smoking?"

He shrugged. "Nothing as earth-shattering as changing my whole life. It just didn't make sense anymore."

"And you don't do anything that doesn't make sense?"

He turned away from her to look into the fire. "Oh, I've been known to do things in my life that don't make sense," he murmured, remembering the times he'd touched her, the kisses and the heat that had flared. He tried to focus and found himself saying something that brought reality in with a thud. "Jonathan Welsh III is part of this new image and new life?"

"Something like that," she said softly.

He watched the way the fire was consuming the logs in the hearth and he knew that what he could feel for Alicia could consume him in the same way. Oddly, at any other time, he would have taken what there was and left. He would have gone and not looked back. But he couldn't with Alicia. She would never be a passing fancy for any man. Especially him.

He shifted back in the chair and glanced at her. She was curled in the corner of the couch like a kitten, her slender fingers worrying a lock of her hair. "So Jon gets the new, reformed Alicia Sullivan?"

Her hand stilled, then slowly let go of her curl. "That's something else I should explain to you. I'm not really engaged."

He felt as if he'd been blindsided. "You aren't going to Jon and his family?"

"Yes, I am, but we're not engaged. He asked me to marry him before he came here, and I said that I'd come just before New Year's and give him my answer. It's . . . it's not official."

He had no right to feel relieved. It shouldn't make any difference to him if she was getting married or not.

"But it will be when you manage to make your way to Jon, won't it?"

"I guess so."

"You don't sound too sure."

"I'm . . . I'm still thinking about it, but I'll probably decide to do it."

"This new life-style isn't so easy, is it?" he asked.

"It's damn hard," she muttered. "You don't have any cigarettes around here, do you?" Before he could answer, she shook her head. "Never mind. I don't want one. I'm just . . . Everything's that's happened makes things so confusing."

"Do you love him?" Steven asked, wondering even as the words came why he uttered them. The last thing he needed was for this woman to tell him that she loved Jon Welsh.

Alicia closed her eyes, trying to shut Buck out of her thoughts by that simple act, anything so she could answer him truthfully. But closing her eyes didn't shut out the fact he was just a few feet from her, or stop the scent of clean maleness and spicy after-shave from touching each breath she took. Or blot out the memory of the kiss and her reaction to it.

"Alicia?"

He said her name softly, and she knew she had to look at him. Slowly she opened her eyes and met his image. The moment she saw Buck, his dark hair swept back from his angular face, she knew the answer to his question. She loved Jon, but not the way she could love Buck if she let herself.

That last thought stopped her dead, and it scared her to death. "No!" she wanted to scream into the air.

"This can't be happening. It won't." She bit her lip hard to center herself, then managed, "Excuse me?"

"Do you love Jon?"

There was no way she could explain things to Buck. *Especially* not to him. "I'm thinking of marrying him," she hedged.

But he didn't let go. "And?"

"He's wonderful. He's smart and a hard worker and he...he...he's so focused, you can't believe it."

"And he's a Welsh, don't forget that."

She could feel the heat in her face, and she hated it. Why was she telling this man all about herself? She still didn't know much about him. "Yes, he's a Welsh." It struck her right then that she had no idea what Buck's last name was. "What are you?" she asked.

"I don't—?"

"Your last name. You never told me what it is."

He sat up, leaning forward to rest his elbows on his knees. His dark lashes shadowed his eyes, making them even more unreadable. "What difference does it make? A name's—" He shook his head. "Forget that. I'm not getting into a discussion about names with you again."

She glanced at the dog, and as if the animal sensed her gaze, he shifted and lolled his head back over his shoulder. His dark eyes met hers, then he shifted, sat up and slowly crossed to the couch. "Pax," she said, reaching out to ruffle his fur as he sat at her feet and dropped his muzzle on her thigh. "Pax. What's in a name? A rose by any other name...?" She looked back at Buck. "What's your name?"

He clasped his hands loosely between his legs, his blue eyes narrowed, studying her intently. "Buck."

"Buck what?"

"Buck Smith."

"Sure it is."

"Take it or leave it."

"Maybe before I leave, you'll do me the favor of telling me the truth."

"You won't be staying that long," he muttered.

Pax shifted to glance back at Buck, then settled against Alicia again with a grunt. "He wants to know, too," she said.

"Sure he does," Buck said as he stood.

For a second, Alicia thought the movement was from Buck standing, then she realized it was happening again. But this time she knew it wasn't an earthquake. Pax moved away from her, looked at Buck and began to howl. Buck moved with a speed that took Alicia's breath away. He had her by the hand, pulling her toward the exit, and she didn't fight him.

In a second they were at the door, Buck had it open, and the roaring outside was deafening. As Buck reached for their jackets, everything stopped. No movement, no rumbling, no howling. Buck stood still, listening, and Alicia held to his hand, waiting.

As cold air tumbled into the room, silence seemed to be everywhere, then Buck slowly swung the door shut. "That didn't sound as close as the first one."

Alicia relished the feeling of his fingers laced with hers, and she didn't try to pull free. She remembered the sight of the first avalanche, the huge chunk of snow that had literally fallen from the peaks, and she wasn't about to let go of Buck. "I've been thinking about something."

"What?"

She looked up at him. "Are you sure you're supposed to go outside when there's an avalanche?"

He looked surprised by the question.

"I mean, wouldn't you stay inside where, if you get buried under tons of snow, you've got an air pocket? That makes sense, doesn't it?"

She didn't know what she expected, but it wasn't Buck laughing, a rich sound that filled the cabin, then pulling her to him in a smothering hug. "You've got a point," he said, his voice a rumble against her cheek.

She spread her hand on his chest over his heart and relished the way she felt surrounded by Buck. His essence was everywhere, and the intimate contact was every bit as potent as the kiss had been earlier. Damn him. Why did he have to smell so good and feel so good, and make her fantasy take flight? Yet she knew she would endure an avalanche anytime if it meant Buck would laugh with her, and hold her, and let her feel his heart beating against her hand.

She looked up at Buck and the minute she looked into his eyes, she knew her mistake. There was no snow in here, no chill all around, no bulky jackets the way there had been earlier. No barriers but two thin shirts— and both his.

Alicia wasn't aware her lips had parted, or that her breathing was racing so much she sounded as if she'd just run a sprint in record time. Not until Buck breathed her name and dipped his head to capture her lips.

Alicia had heard about instant, primal passion, but she'd never believed in it until that moment. She'd never believed that emotions could transform into white-hot desire simply by one person touching another person. And she'd been wrong. The moment Buck touched his lips to hers, the moment she felt his body against hers, his arms around her, she was lost.

She opened her mouth, welcoming his thrusting invasion, and she wrapped her arms around his neck, willing herself to be closer to him than was humanly possible. Her body throbbed with life, and when Buck kissed a fiery path to her throat, she moaned with pleasure. When his hands tugged at the shirt and the top button popped, she moved enough to undo the other buttons. And when his hands found her breasts and when they cupped them, his thumbs caressing her nipples through the thin lace of her bra, she lost the ability to breathe.

Pleasure, pure and simple. Fire and honey. Joy that knew no bounds. And when he lifted her into his arms and carried her to the couch, she held on for dear life. She never wanted to let go. She never wanted this to end. The leather felt cool on her flushed skin as Buck lowered her onto the cushions, then he was over her, and she looked up at him.

She saw, reflected in him, the fire that burned in her, and with unsteady fingers, she undid the buttons on his shirt. Then she pushed back the cotton, and she felt the sleek heat of his skin under her hands. The muscles in his abdomen were tense, and his breathing was rapid and shallow. With exquisite gentleness, he pushed aside her shirt and looked down at her.

"God, you're beautiful," he rasped. Then his fingers hooked under her bra and tugged it up until her breasts spilled out, free of the confines of the lace.

Skin against skin, and the contact was overwhelming for Alicia. Never had she felt a touch that she knew went straight to her soul. Never had she felt a touch that drew on something so primal in her that her instincts were to wantonly offer everything she had. Never had she felt a touch that brought to her an ache that was the perfect blend of pain and pleasure.

Buck lowered his head, and his lips replaced his hands, his tongue teasing her nipples, and she arched back in the couch. "Yes," she breathed, her fingers clenching the fabric of his shirt so tightly they were numb. "Oh, yes," she groaned, and as his lips moved lower, to the rise and fall of her stomach, dipping close to the brief bikini panties, she could feel tears on her cheeks.

She pushed her hands under his shirt, and around to the width of his back. She skimmed her hands over his skin, relishing the strength she felt there, then as she moved her hand down, she felt the gun. Right then she heard the barking, and the haze of pleasure began to dissolve. She was blind, letting herself get carried away. But the feel of cold steel, and the barking of the dog, shattered her insanity in one fell swoop.

What was she doing? She felt Buck move back from her, and she looked up at him, his eyes lingering on her exposed breasts. Killing the urge to cover herself, she felt cold all around her and in her. A fool. That's what she was. Rushing in where angels fear to tread. Even a fool would know better than to do what she almost did.

Buck watched her, his expression tightening, as if he knew her thoughts. Then he moved away from her. "I need to go and see what's out there," he said, his voice as unsteady as she felt at the moment.

There were no apologies, no promises, no demand for an explanation, just a silent glance that was unreadable before he left her. The cool air touched her exposed skin, and she grasped at the sides of her shirt, tugging them across her breasts as she rolled to one side to sit up on the couch.

Buck stood to get his jacket, and there was no way to hide the evidence of his desire. The jeans were tested, and she looked away, holding the shirt together at her throat. If the dog hadn't barked, if she hadn't felt the gun, she would have acted on her feelings, on her impulses. She never learned. Never. Never.

She closed her eyes, and didn't open them again until she heard the door close behind Buck.

In that second after he left, she knew a totally irrational need to go after him. But she didn't. She was sensible. She acted like a mature adult and saved herself from making a horrendous mistake.

"Damn you, Buck," she muttered to herself as she stared at the door. None of her sensible maturity completely killed her lingering need for the man. It didn't take away that coiled knot in her middle, or stop the trembling in her hands. She made fists, sank back in the couch and nibbled on her lip. "What I wouldn't give for a cigarette right now."

Sampson sat on the ground at the Denver Airport in the private jet, waiting for his transportation to Gibson. Out the window he could see snow had blanketed the city all around, and word was the storm had hit hardest near Gibson.

He glanced at his notes on the tray in front of him. "Phones and electricity are out, and the road crews are barely making a dent in clearing the access roads around Gibson," he read to himself.

He looked at his watch. Two o'clock. It would probably be dark before he could even think about getting to Rider. As he glanced up, he saw the first flakes of snow touch the glass of the window. "Damn it all," he muttered, then turned and called to the agent near the door. "Get on the horn and get weather for the next twelve hours."

He looked back at the window with the snow streaking it. If another storm was coming in, it could be tomorrow before he made contact. He sank back in the chair. Word was the trial would resume the day after New Year's. They had the jury, the opening statements had been made and technical witnesses had been called. If he got Rider out tomorrow, he'd have to find another place to wait. Some place Sabbo didn't know anything about.

He could just keep him in the plane, circling until it was time for his testimony, if he had to. No hit man could get to him up in the air. Or maybe he'd just get Rider in the car and drive until it was time for him to show at the court. There was always a contingency plan. Although Sabbo knew that, the best thing was, he didn't know what contingency plans Sampson used these days.

Jaimie L. strode through the airport in Denver. Gibson, Colorado. He'd never heard of it before last night. Fact was, the only cities he'd heard of in Colorado were Denver and Aspen. He moved through the holiday crowd to get to the car rental counter and stepped behind a man talking to the counter person. When the man stepped aside, Jaimie L. took his place and smiled at the woman when she looked at him.

"Name's Donnagon, Kenneth Donnagon. I've got a reservation."

She worked the computer, then looked at him. "Yes, sir. It's ready for you. We just need to see your credit card and license and we're all set."

"Can you tell me how to get to Gibson?" he asked.

"Yes, sir. It's north of here on the main highway. You can't miss it. Lots of signs on the way. If you're here for the skiing, you've struck gold. At least, you will in a day or two."

"Why a day or two?"

As she motioned behind him, he turned, and through the sheets of glass he could see the terminals and runways. Light snow was falling. "When the snow stops, the conditions should be perfect."

This delayed things a bit, but as long as he could get to Gibson without Sampson knowing about it, he wouldn't have a problem getting to Rider when the weather let up. As long as he was close by, the rest would fall into place. "When I'm ready, I'm sure the conditions will be perfect," he murmured as he signed the rental forms.

Chapter 10

Alicia had never felt so restless or so claustrophobic in her life. Every time she turned around, Buck was there. With every breath she took, she seemed to inhale the scents that clung to him. And every time they accidentally touched, she remembered touches that had been deliberate, that had had a purpose.

The cabin was growing smaller and smaller all the time. She made herself sit on the couch and pick up one of the books Buck had offered her earlier. She flipped it open and stared at the words, but all she could think about was the man moving around behind the closed door of the bathroom. She heard the water running, a thudding when he dropped something, then silence. Subconsciously she braced herself as the door clicked and opened.

The words on the pages blurred as she heard Buck coming out, walking across the floor, then the drawer to the dresser sliding open. She closed the book, giving up on ever knowing what it said. As wind shook the windows, she looked up and saw the snow was still falling, lightly and softly. Nothing like the blizzard of yesterday.

"Have you checked the phone?"

Buck's voice came from just behind Alicia, and she barely controlled her surprise. She stared at the closed book on her lap. "It's still out."

Alicia saw Pax stir, then, with a sigh, get up and go to the door. He scratched at the wood, then looked over his shoulder in the direction of Buck and Alicia.

"I know, I know, Pax," Buck murmured as he crossed to the door. Alicia watched the way he moved, the long strides, the way the fresh jeans molded to his thighs, the white cotton of the plain T-shirt hugging his shoulders and chest. His hair was still damp from the shower, skimmed back from his face, and his feet were bare.

"Just like a teenager," she chided herself silently. *"Look at him and forget how to breathe."*

"You want out. Be my guest," Buck said as he opened the barrier. "I'm not falling for that 'someone's out there' look this time." Even though the growing breeze drifted snow into the cabin, the dog didn't hesitate to go outside. Buck swung the door shut, crossed to the fireplace, and as he put a heavy log on the grate, Alicia noticed that the gun wasn't in the back of his waistband.

"Where's the gun?" she asked.

Buck pulled the screen back over the fire and stood. Then he turned to her, and she knew she was having trouble breathing as she watched him move. She was almost completely incapable of taking a normal breath with him looking at her. "I put it away."

"Good." She looked back down at the book she was gripping so tightly that her knuckles were white. Making a conscious effort to relax her hands, she flexed her fingers and smoothed them across the jacket of the book. "I've always hated guns."

"Sometimes they're necessary."

"I guess you'd know, what with being a bodyguard." She tossed the book to the cushions on the couch by her and leaned back, closing her eyes. "My sister got shot at last year during that Terrine thing. She wasn't really hit, but the bullet tore her blouse and almost hit her in the arm. It scared me to death."

She heard him move, then the chair squeaked as he sat down. It seemed safer for her to keep her eyes closed.

"And you decided to change your life right then?"

"Bingo—give the man a cigar." He chuckled, a soft sound that ran havoc over her frayed nerves.

"A cigarette . . . if I have my choice."

"Unless you're hiding some around here, the closest you're going to get is wishing."

"You can't get in trouble just wishing."

Oh, yes she could. If she could wish for one thing right now, it wouldn't be for a cigarette. And the trouble that could come to her, if she let herself wish for the impossible, was disturbing. So she said what she knew she should be wishing for right now. "I'd be happy just to get the phone working, or to have the snow stop, or get the roads cleared." But she knew the magnitude of the lies even before those words were out.

"I thought you'd wish to get to Jon."

She opened her eyes and saw Buck at the window with his back to her, looking outside. "Of course," she murmured, adding lie upon lie. Needing a diversion, she asked, "When the snow stops and the roads clear, where are you going?"

He didn't turn to her. "To look for work."

"As a bodyguard?"

"I don't think so. That phase of my life's over."

"So what sort of work will you try to get?"

He shrugged, straining the cotton of his shirt across his shoulders. "Something that makes money." He turned. "I'm not the son of a banker, so it's up to me to do what I need to do. It's always been like that."

She remembered what he'd said about his parents. "You've been on your own for a long time, haven't you?"

"Since I was sixteen."

"You left home?"

"I walked out. I was fed up with my father, and I knew if I stayed, I'd be pulling him up out of the gutter for the rest of my life or I'd kill him." He raked his fingers through his hair, skimming it back from his high-cheekboned face. His eyes were narrowed, his expression giving away no emotion, even though Alicia knew he must have gone through a lot of pain when he'd left. "So I took off."

"Where did you go?"

"Away. I got a job as a cook. Then a guy in the restaurant asked if I'd ever done construction work. I lied and told him I had, and I got on a crew that was going to work on homes in Florida."

As Buck spoke, Alicia had the niggling suspicion that although he came from a different place, a different background, his way of getting through life was uncomfortably like hers had been. "Did it work out?"

"Sure. I watched, listened and copied. That's a secret I learned first thing. If someone around you knows what they're doing, you've got it made."

"Then what did you do?"

"This and that. I worked on a ranch for a while, worked in some schooling for myself, and even did some movie work as an extra." He smiled ruefully. "They thought I had the look of an Indian."

"Are you part Indian?"

He shook his head. "No. My mother was Irish and my father was Italian."

"Smith's an Italian name?"

He laughed at that. "It is if I say it is."

She wasn't going to touch that, not now. She just wanted to hear him talk, to learn about him and his past. "How did you get to be a bodyguard?"

"I was working at a health club in Phoenix, and one of the clients asked if I'd ever done bodyguard work. I asked why he was asking, and he mentioned a friend who had a full-time bodyguard, but needed some extra protection for a few months."

"And let me guess. You told him you did that sort of work all the time?"

"Bingo."

"And you watched and learned, and you had a career."

His expression tightened. "I had a job for two months. He recommended me to another friend in Dallas. I stayed there for six months, then I got a job in Houston."

The fire popped and sent a shower of sparks up the chimney, startling Alicia. She'd been mesmerized talking to Buck, the world as distant from her as Gibson was from this cabin. As he filled in the blanks of his life, she realized she could almost fill them in herself before he spoke the words. His life seemed to be an echo of hers in so many ways. "So, is there a license or something you get to protect people?"

There was a scratch at the door. "I don't even have a diploma," he said as he went to the door and opened it. The dog came inside. Pax glanced at Alicia as he went directly to the fireplace. Steven closed the door then crossed to his chair. He sank down in the cushions and asked, "Do they give diplomas for blackjack dealing?"

She shook her head. "No, and not for waitresses, or receptionists, or tour guides, or clerks in video stores."

"Your past?"

"A bit of it. The better jobs."

"How did you get to be a blackjack dealer?"

She settled deeper in the corner of the sofa. "I lucked into it. No pun intended. I was in Las Vegas and when I answered an ad for sharing an apartment, the girl worked at the casino. They needed dealers, and she taught me how to do it." She exhaled. "She bailed out on me about a month later and left me holding the bag for the rent. But I made good tips and was getting along pretty well . . . until I met Mick Terrine. That really messed up things."

"What does Jon think about Terrine?"

That startled her. "He never actually said."

"You never told him?"

"Of course I did." She closed her eyes and could almost hear the conversation they'd had after she'd told him about the Las Vegas fiasco.

"Thank goodness you're out of that life," Jon had said, never uttering the name Terrine. *"Bad choices are a thing of the past. From now on, those sorts aren't part of your life."*

But he'd made her life sound sordid, and for a moment she'd felt resentful toward the life Jon had led—protected and privileged. Then, as he'd smiled at her, she'd forgotten all about it. *"What counts is now,"* he'd told her, *"and us. No one else."*

"And how did he take it?" Buck asked.

She opened her eyes and stared at the fire. "He understood. It was over. I wasn't about to repeat those mistakes again."

"There are other sorts of mistakes in this world besides bad judgment," Buck said.

She shrugged. "I guess so, but it seems that when I've got a choice, I make the wrong one...at least fifty percent of the time. Jon wanted to meet me in Denver and drive out here with me, but I told him, 'No, I'll do just fine.' Then this happens."

"Why didn't you want him to meet you?"

She spoke without thinking. "It made me feel as if I didn't have a choice, as if... I don't know."

"As if you were trapped, that you didn't have any options. Maybe stifled?"

She looked at Buck, shocked that he'd described exactly how Jon's offer had made her feel. "Maybe," she hedged.

"A bit of advice?"

She didn't speak.

"Rethink this marriage proposal. If him offering to drive you to the house makes you feel like that, what's marriage going to do to you?"

She got to her feet. "Just a minute, I never said that I didn't want to be married. Don't try and read your own interpretation into all of this. Just because of...of things that have happened recently doesn't mean that I don't want to be married."

He looked up at her. "Things?"

Her face felt like fire. "Things," she muttered.

"All right. Things. Just remember how you felt about a drive—think about how you'll feel about a lifetime."

"And you're an expert? I thought you said you'd never been married."

Buck stood, coming to within just a few feet of Alicia. "Trust me," he said. "That's why I've never been married. I know what I'm talking about. Every time I even had a passing thought about anything like that, I broke out in hives." Unexpectedly, he tapped her chin with his finger. "When you see Jon again, tell him you talk to yourself, you make snow angels and you make perfect snowballs."

She froze at the contact, swallowing hard when he glanced at her lips, then back to her eyes. For a moment she was terrified he'd kiss her again. And she couldn't take it. The percentage of times she'd made bad decisions had gone up dramatically since they'd met, and she wasn't about to let that percentage go up any farther.

She touched her tongue to her lips. "Jon knows all he needs to know about me."

"You'd better check for hives next time you see him," he said, then turned away. "I'll get more wood before it gets too dark."

While he got dressed and headed for the door, Alicia came to grips with what could happen if Buck touched her or even looked at her. God, if the snow would only stop and the roads were cleared, she could get out of here before she did something she knew she'd live to regret.

"Why don't you start some coffee?" Buck said as he opened the door, letting the dog go out first. "I'll be right back with the wood."

He closed the door behind him and stayed on the porch for several minutes. Treacherous. Being confined in the cabin with Alicia was definitely treacherous. Every time he got close to her, or touched her, he knew how deep his emotions were for a woman he'd known for such a short time.

The image of her under him on the couch, her breasts exposed, her lips parted... He hit the post of the porch with the flat of his hand so hard that snow tumbled off the roof and landed softly in the drifts. He'd been crazy to let that happen. He should have known it would happen, but that didn't excuse it.

If there wasn't a Jon. If they'd met before all this with Shaw. If he... The thought completed and brought him actual pain in his midsection. If he had anything to offer Alicia. But he didn't, neither a name nor a life.

He crossed the porch, barely noticing that the snow was letting up. The dog led the way toward the lean-to, and Steven followed Pax, his chin tucked into his jacket, his hair lifting in the wind. Damn it all. He had to focus. He had to concentrate on what he needed to do, not on what he wished he could do.

One thing he could do was walk to her car and see what she had there. He veered off the path to the lean-to and started toward the road. Maybe if he knew more about her, he could make more sense out of what he *had* to do.

The trip to Gibson was long and tedious for Sampson. The speed limit was thirty miles per hour because of the slick new snow falling on the recently cleared roads. He didn't look at the landscape as he drove the four-by-four sedan and spoke into the cellular phone.

"Any word on Jaimie L.?"

The agent on the other end of the line said, "Not a word. No one's seen him. No one's heard from him or about him."

It was as if he'd dropped off the face of the earth, but Sampson wasn't counting on it. His gut instinct was that Shaw would get to Rider someway, somehow. He wouldn't sit back and just let things happen. And people like Jaimie L. were there to see that every option was executed—in every sense of the word.

Sampson barely glanced at the village of Gibson as he approached it. The grayness of the day seemed to hover over it, making the bright wooden signs almost mocking. "What's the reading?"

"Roads are being cleared, but it might take the rest of the day and tonight before you get access. High winds, but no more storms in the forecast."

Sampson slowed as he drove onto the main street. "Where am I staying?"

"Crystal Mountain Chalet."

As the man said it over the line, Sampson spotted the hotel. A discreet structure, blending into the ruggedness of the surroundings, all stone and wood and blanketed with snow. "I'm here. Contact me if there's anything new. I'll let you know what's happening on this end."

He put the phone back in the holder and realized they should have left a cellular with Rider. He'd never thought of it before, and he could kick himself now. Simple. Elementary. And completely overlooked.

He waited for a black Jeep with tinted windows to pull out of the parking lot of a small shopping center on the right, then drove behind it toward the hotel. He swung into the driveway of the hotel and stopped at the front doors. "A cellular phone," he muttered as he picked his up and got out of the car. "Newfangled invention that could have saved a hell of a lot of work and worry."

Alicia couldn't sit still. In the quietness of the empty cabin, she paced back and forth, wishing one minute for the ability to get to Jon, and in the next that she could stay here forever. If she had space, if she could get someplace where she could think, maybe she could make sense out of what was happening to her.

She crossed the room, past the fireplace, and looked out the window. As if an answer of sorts had come, the lead-gray sky looked heavy with clouds, but no more snow was falling. She turned and went to the phone by the couch. Picking up the receiver, she listened, but there was still nothing but silence.

She dropped the receiver. "One thing at a time. The snow stopping is a good start." She looked around the cabin, then remembered what Buck had asked when he left. "Coffee," she muttered. She'd completely forgotten.

She headed for the kitchen and stopped as she entered the room. "Coffee? Coffee? Where would I be if I was a can or jar of coffee?" She looked in the pantry but couldn't find any coffee.

She turned, saw the coffeepot on the stove, and went across to the cabinets by the stove. She opened the nearest door and found a can of coffee on the top shelf. Quickly she got it out and opened it, but there wasn't a ladle in it. Setting the can on the counter, she opened the drawers by the cupboard. The top drawer was empty except for some papers, the top one titled *Rental Agreement.*

She almost closed the drawer, but her eye caught the name on the papers, *Joseph Riley.* Probably the renter before Buck, she thought, but when she glanced at the dates of the rental period, she knew she was wrong— December 15 of this year was the beginning date, and the ending date was open but not to exceed forty-five days.

She picked up the top sheet. The home address was in Chicago. Age of applicant: 37. Number of occupants in rental: one. Employer: Mann Engineering. Length of employment: 7 years. She flipped it over and saw a signature of agreement—Joseph Riley.

She looked back in the drawer and saw an envelope. Putting the paper down, she took out the envelope, lifted the unsealed flap and slid the contents out onto the counter. Right on top was an ID card for Mann Engineering with a laminated color picture of Buck on it. The name Joseph Riley was typed under it, and on a line up the side, the signature, the same as on the rental agreement.

In the same envelope was an Illinois driver's license, an ATM card and two credit cards in the same name. The signatures matched the others, and Buck's picture was on both the driver's license and one of the credit cards. Alicia touched the employment ID, annoyed that her finger was unsteady.

She felt as if she'd been hit in the gut. "It was all lies. All lies. He just made up a life." Her stomach knotted. "And I thought I was seeing the real him." He'd seemed so honest talking to her, as if he was finally letting her get a glimpse of the man himself.

The man he wanted her to see, was more like it. She quickly pushed everything back in the envelope and put it and the form back in the drawer. With a low "That's it," she slammed the drawer shut and went back into the living room.

"What do I care if he's Buck Smith or Joe Riley?" she breathed as she went to get her clothes from the hearth. She didn't want to feel his shirt on her skin any longer. What had moments ago been comforting and soft, felt like a straitjacket now.

"I don't give a damn who he is. I'll just get out of here and away from him as soon as I can." She crossed to the bathroom and went inside, slamming the door behind her.

In five minutes she was dressed and back out in the living room. She threw Buck's shirt onto the couch, then dropped down on the leather and reached for the phone.

"How can I be such a bad judge of men?" she demanded, refusing to look directly at how close she had come to messing up her life again. "From day one, I get mixed up with the Mick Terrines of this world, and now Buck or Joe, or whatever his name is."

The receiver was dead in her hands, and she put it back in the cradle so hard she could hear the vibrating impact of plastic on plastic. She'd have given anything to get out of here before Buck came back, but she didn't have a chance. The car was stuck, and walking to Jon's would be out of the question.

She hugged her arms around herself and glared at the front door. "Come on, come on," she muttered. "Whoever you are." Then, as if her words had conjured him up, she heard his footsteps on the porch.

Jaimie L. wasn't a patient man. He stood at the window of his hotel room and stared down at the main street of Gibson. A hole in the wall. Nowhere. It might be pricey and a place to be seen, but give him New York, or even Houston, any day over this place.

The snow had finally stopped, but getting out of town into the foothills was impossible until morning. And he knew others were here. The government wasn't exactly stupid, although he wondered about their intelligence when Rider was deposited alone to wait. No bodyguards. No protection at all.

The phone rang, and Jaimie L. crossed the room to grab the receiver. "Yeah?"

"What's the order?"

"A special."

"That'll cost."

"I'll pay."

"All right. It'll be delivered in an hour to the front desk. Roses are hard to come by this time of year around here, so leave instructions that the flowers are to be sent up to your room the minute they arrive."

"Of course."

He pressed the disconnect button, feeling better now that he knew he'd have the gun tonight. Then he pushed the number his contact with Shaw had given him. The line was picked up after two rings, but no one said hello. "The deadline is nine tomorrow morning."

"Contact me at ten."

"Just have the roll ready."

"Verification is required."

"That's the agreement," Jaimie L. muttered, hating the "suit squad," as he called the men that circled Shaw.

The line buzzed in his ear, and he put the receiver down with a thud. He wouldn't charge for taking out one of Shaw's goons, just for practice.

He'd seen Rider at Shaw's that one time. He didn't dislike him, but then again, he didn't like him, either. And that made a good business deal. No emotions. When you hated people, you screwed up. He couldn't remember the last person he really hated. Then he remembered. Sampson. Yes, he hated him. Maybe that was why the idea of eliminating someone Sampson was protecting appealed to him. Either way, Rider was going to be dead.

Chapter 11

Steven walked into the cabin, and the presence of Alicia was as potent as anything he'd ever experienced in his life. The moment he saw her, the world narrowed to just her. Her flame-colored hair that curled so brilliantly, her green eyes and porcelain skin, the elegant line of her throat. She seemed to surround him, her essence filling him, and he wasn't even close enough to touch her.

He closed the door to the cold and coming night, and he'd taken off his leather jacket and boots before he realized he'd been so intent on the effect Alicia had on him, that he hadn't been aware something was wrong.

He looked around the room, uneasiness making him wish he hadn't left the gun in the dresser drawer. But nothing looked out of place. As he went to check the fire, he looked at Alicia again and knew what was wrong. She looked angry. She sat ramrod straight on the edge of the couch cushions, her arms folded over her breasts, her lips compressed in a straight line. A defensive posture if ever he'd seen one.

"What's going on?" He darted a look at the phone. "Is the phone working?"

"No."

The coldness outside was nothing compared to the ice in her voice. Then he thought he understood. "It's the dog, isn't it? I know he's not with me. He took off, just like he did the last time. And there's no point in going out to look for him. He'll show up." Her expression wasn't changing. The anger was still there. "I'm not going after the animal. Trust me, he'll be back when he wants to come back, if he wants to come back."

"His name is Pax, and it's not him."

"Then what is it? I refuse to have a fight with you if I don't even know why you're mad."

She looked up at him, and even those elegant long lashes couldn't soften the strength of her expression. "I know who you are."

He tried to control the adrenaline rush that flooded over him. *She knew.* The world tipped out of control. There had been nothing in the car. The rental agreement had been in her name, and it had the L.A. address. It all looked legitimate, and it had let him forget about the glimmer of suspicion that she wasn't here by chance.

"Of course you do," he said, holding on to his control while he bluffed, hoping against hope she wasn't saying what he thought she was saying.

"I know who you *really* are," she said, and he could see the tension in her jaw as she uttered each word.

He forced himself not to glance at the dresser as he wondered if he could get to the gun before she could act. But he gave up the idea almost immediately. He knew she didn't have any weapon with her—except her own presence. And there hadn't been any weapons in the car.

"All right. I give up. Who am I?"

She shifted, clenching her hands together on her lap, and her eyes never left his face. "Joseph Riley from Chicago, Illinois."

He felt light-headed with relief, quickly followed by self-anger. If he needed any solid evidence of how Alicia affected him, this was it. His cover story. Someway she'd found out about it. He should have just said he was Joe Riley, said it as easily as he could have said his real name. He shouldn't have pulled a blank and come up with the name Buck. His only excuse was that everything about Alicia surprised him and kept him off balance. Even his thought process was out of whack.

He regrouped and tried to smile, to lighten the mood in some way while he thought about a plausible explanation for his slipup. "Is that what this is all about?"

"Damn it, it's not funny. This isn't a joke. You lied to me."

He sobered. "I know it's not a joke." Anything that could make him feel so disoriented certainly wasn't funny. "But I can explain about the name thing."

"Can you explain about the past *thing,* and the job *thing,* that story about being a bodyguard?"

If he was lucky, he could come up with lies to cover the lies, but he wasn't prepared for how the idea of lying to Alicia again made him feel. His middle was in a huge knot. "I know how important names are to you, but—"

She stood abruptly, almost bumping into him, and he backed up, not wanting contact with her while he was trying to think straight enough to get himself out of this mess. He thought she was going to pass him and give him much-needed space. But she didn't.

Instead, she squared around to face him. Before he could do or say anything, she uttered a shattering oath that would have made any sailor proud, and the next thing he knew, she punched him squarely in the jaw.

If it had been anyone else who hit him, Steven knew he would have struck back and struck hard. But not Alicia. Even when she pushed him with the flats of her hands on his chest and sent him reeling back onto the couch, he didn't fight back. His jaw hurt like hell, but he didn't try to get up. He leaned against the leather cushions, surprised that he wasn't seeing stars or tasting blood.

He flexed his jaw carefully and asked, "What in the hell was that for?"

Alicia stood over him, shaking her right hand. "For lying to me like that. I hate liars," she breathed in an unsteady voice.

Her explosive anger he could deal with, even the punch, but there was no way he could handle the brightness of tears beginning to shine in her eyes or the way her bottom lip trembled. Before he could figure out something to stop the pain he knew his lies had caused, she spun on her heels and headed into the kitchen. He heard her rummaging around, then the slam of a drawer, and she came back into the room with an envelope in her hand. Without looking at

Steven, she emptied the contents of the envelope onto the coffee table.

He looked down and saw a driver's license, a couple of credit cards and what looked like an employee ID card. She'd found the packet Sampson had left for his cover. He looked at an older picture of himself on the employment ID, and cringed. No wonder she thought he was the liar of the year.

"Where did you find these?" he asked without looking at her, knowing the answer, but needing the time to think.

"In the drawer by the stove. That's you, isn't it?"

"Would you believe my identical twin?"

"Can't you ever give me a straight answer?"

He looked up at her and saw the tears dampening her face. She didn't move to wipe them off or acknowledge them in any way. She just stood very still, her chin unsteady but high, and despite the control she was keeping, she looked incredibly vulnerable. It tore at him. "Alicia, I never meant for anyone to be involved in this, let alone you. I never thought you'd turn up in the snow half-frozen to death." And he never expected to fall in love with a woman who couldn't be any more than a memory when he left this place.

Love? The strength of that realization left him fighting to take his next breath. This wasn't love. It couldn't be. Not when Steven Rider only had a few more days to exist. Yet he knew no matter how much he denied it, it wouldn't change what he felt right now.

"Who are you?" she asked, her voice so low he almost couldn't hear her.

"I wish I could explain everything."

"Just tell me who you are."

He fought for something—anything—to say, but there was nothing he could tell her that wouldn't be a lie. He reached out, and ignoring her flinch, he caught her by her shoulders with both hands. He was vaguely surprised that she didn't fight him, trying to get away from him holding her. But she didn't. She stood motionless, her face damp, her lashes spiked with tears and her skin startlingly pale. "I can't tell you anything."

Her tongue touched her pale lips. "Why?"

She felt so slight under his hands, and a faint trembling in her shoulders was almost his undoing. "I'm sorry. I can't tell you that, either."

"I'm sorry, too," she whispered.

"Alicia, my life's been crazy. What I told you before was the truth. About my parents, about my leaving home and the jobs. I probably told you more about myself than I've ever told anyone before."

"You don't have to lie anymore," she said.

"That's not a lie," he whispered, and as he looked into her green eyes, he knew with a heart-wrenching certainty that it wasn't a lie, that after thirty-seven years his brief time with Alicia was the very best his life had ever been. And as he looked down at her, he knew it was the best it would ever be.

Alicia had long ago felt the anger drain from her. And a deep aching pain had begun to grow in her. Tears fell from her eyes, the heat trickling down her cheeks, but all she could think of was being betrayed. A man she hadn't known existed just days ago, had become the center of her universe and had the ability to hurt her beyond anything she could have ever imagined.

Others she'd known had made her mad, they'd frustrated her and even frightened her, but none had made her feel this pain. She hated Buck for that, and she hated herself for letting it happen. When he'd stood and faced her, when he'd touched her, she'd known how deeply that pain went. No one in her life had ever bruised her soul...not until Buck. Not until he'd touched her, kissed her, and made her believe in the idea that love could come in a flash of brilliance.

The thought made the pain deepen. Love. She'd never known it before. But she understood that now. And she had never suspected that it could hurt this much. "Please, you don't have to do this," she managed around the growing tightness in her throat.

"I know I don't." His hold on her tightened a bit. "But I want you to believe me that I would have never lied to you unless I had to." A smile flitted uncertainly around the corners of his mouth. "And if you want to hit me again, go ahead. I deserve it."

She lifted an unsteady hand and touched his jaw. "I'm sorry. I've never hit anyone in my life." She felt the bristling of a new beard under her fingertips and the heat of his skin. "I was just so mad, I..." She drew back. "I just... Lies make me feel..." She couldn't put words together at all.

"Believe me, this isn't a lie," Buck murmured, and drew her to him.

His arms closed around her, and she felt lost in the sensation of safety and comfort. It could all be an illusion, and it could go up in a puff of smoke at any time, but she couldn't let it go. She pressed her hands flat on his chest, then rested her head on it and closed her eyes.

"This, right now, right here, is not a lie," he whispered. "But it's all I can give you. There can't be any more."

She heard his words, and she knew right then that she would take whatever he could give her, as little or as much as he could offer. And she wanted it. She loved him. It was just that simple and that complicated.

His hand cupped her chin and gently lifted her head until she had to look at him. "Do you understand?" he asked, the heat of his breath fanning her face.

She understood that she loved this man with a single-mindedness that she'd never experienced before. That that love had come to her with a suddenness that rivaled a bolt of lightning. And she understood that there was no way she could walk away from him tonight. There was no one else. There never had been. There never could be.

"Do you understand?" he repeated, his voice low and vibrating with intensity.

"Yes," she breathed, and knew she understood so much now that she hadn't just a heartbeat ago. And it didn't surprise her at all that one night with Buck was worth a lifetime with anyone else.

One night. The phrase chanted in her mind, and when Buck drew her back to him, she felt a desperation in her that came from nowhere to possess her. One night. That was all, and she knew she didn't want to waste a second of it.

When Buck kissed her, she clung to him, needing more and wanting it desperately. She wanted everything, and she wanted it now. She wound her arms around his neck, sinking her fingers in his hair, and she pressed against Buck. If she could, she would have melted right into him, become a part of him forever and never have a breath of distance between them.

She sensed the same urgency in Buck, in the way he caressed her, the way his lips tasted her closed eyes and found the pulse by her ear. She fumbled with the buttons on his shirt. Once it was undone, she pushed the cotton back and off his shoulders. He shrugged out of it, tossing it behind him, and she touched her finger to the hollow of his throat. As she traced a line on his chest, downward, over the suggestion of dark hair, to the waistband of his jeans, he muttered an impatient oath and caught the hem of her sweater.

In one swift movement, he tugged the white wool up and over her head, then sent it flying back over his head in the same general direction the shirt had gone moments before. For an eternity, he looked at her, his eyes filled with hunger, then he had her in his arms, lifting her high while he carried her to the bedroom.

As he laid her on the bed, she pulled him with her and they tumbled together onto the linen. The urgency that had been there before grew into a frantic need in Alicia. There was no gradual building of passion, no flickering flame that slowly grew to a fire, but an instant inferno. His hands found her waistband, undid the button, and her slacks were gone before she knew it.

As his fingers brushed her stomach, she tightened and felt as if she were being set on fire from the inside out. "Buck," she breathed, and closed her eyes as the tips of his fingers worked their way under the elastic of her panties.

With the world shut out, all Alicia knew was what she felt, how Buck touched her, where he touched her.

When he eased her panties off, she lifted her hips to help free them. Then they were gone, and she felt Buck lay his hand on her thigh. He ran his fingers along her skin, to the point of her hip, across her flat stomach, to her other hip, then down, but when he didn't touch her core, she opened her eyes.

She looked at Buck, who was on his elbow, his eyes watching her face, his expression one of pleasure. He dipped his head to touch his lips to her forehead, then trailed to her mouth. And the kiss was deep and searing—soul-stealing. Commitment came in many forms in this life, but Alicia had never realized that a kiss could be as binding an agreement as a legal document.

She loved him. She opened her mouth wide, savoring the taste filling her. She loved him. His hand stroked her thighs, and her legs opened of their own volition. As the feathery strokes came closer to her center, she wrapped her arms around Buck, holding on to him for dear life. Her teeth ground against his, and she wished that she could inhale him, take every atom of his being into her.

She felt him pressing against her, hot and hard, and that only made her own needs increase. And when his mouth left hers and started its own path downward, she gasped and bit her lip to keep from crying out from the sensations that were bombarding her. She threw her head back as his mouth found the hollow of her throat, then the cleft between her breasts.

His tongue teased her nipples, first one and then the other, hardening them into incredibly sensitive buds, and her breasts swelled toward this caress. When he tasted the hollow at her navel, the rippling muscles of her abdomen, she forgot how to breathe. She braced herself, waiting, wanting, needing. And she lifted her hips, giving him access. And when she thought she'd die if she didn't feel him against her moist heat, he found her bud, and the world exploded into pleasures that knew no bounds.

The sensations rocketed through her, exploding over and over again, and she cried out. When his mouth left her, his hand took its place and he moved the heel of his palm back and forth, up and down, mimicking the stroking that she was crying out for. And just when she felt her sanity slipping, her need for him drowning her, he left her.

She cried out, "No, please," and opened her eyes. Buck was there, standing by the bed, tugging his jeans off, and for a moment he stood there in his briefs. She remembered the first time she saw him like that, his tanned skin dark and sensuous against the pure white cotton. And this time the sight made her heart lurch.

He wanted her. She could see the evidence of that need straining against the cotton, then the briefs were gone, and she gasped. There was no embarrassment, no coyness, just a burning need to feel him inside her, to know him completely, and she held out her arms to him.

He needed no other invitation, and he was with her in the bed again. He was over her, his hair falling forward, the fire of passion in his eyes. She felt him at the cradle of her hips, his strength hot and hard against her, and she gripped him by his shoulders. Digging her fingers into his flesh, she lifted her hips, and she could barely speak. "Please, please," she gasped.

He braced himself over her with his hands flat on the pillow by her head, and he didn't move. When she tried to pull him down, to draw her into him, he moved closer, testing her. "You want this, don't you?" he rasped.

More than life itself, she wanted to say, but all she could manage was a whispered "Yes."

Buck groaned, a low, almost animalistic sound. She felt him test her, his silky strength, touching and stroking, then he entered her. Slowly, ever so slowly, heat and strength, and when she couldn't bear it any longer, she wrapped her legs around his hips and arched toward him.

And he filled her, completely and totally. Neither person moved for a single heartbeat, then Buck began to move, rocking his hips against hers at first, building the momentum. Then he drew back, almost out of her, and for a moment she thought he was leaving her. In the next second, he thrust deeply into her, and desire knew no bounds. Hot and hungry, all-encompassing, her body moved in perfect unison with his.

Faster and faster, higher and higher, until Alicia felt her soul fragment, exploding into a shimmering mass of pure ecstasy. Wave after wave shook her, each one stronger than the last, overlapping, blending into a bliss so intense that she felt if she let go of Buck, she'd soar into the sky and disappear.

She heard her name come from him, a low rasping whisper filled with the same intensity that she was experiencing, and she opened her eyes. Buck was over her, his face tensed with the strength of his emotions, and she knew that she would never love another man like this again. She'd never know this completeness, this joining again, and eternity seemed too short a time to lie with him.

He thrust deeper and deeper, and as he looked down at her, she exploded into a world of unreality, a place where sensations were everything. Darkness hovered on the edges, and feelings were almost painful. Then she heard him utter her name, and she was lost. Wave after wave of sensations rode through her, and at the same moment she knew she couldn't bear it any longer, she climaxed into a place that had never existed before for her. A place where only Buck could take her.

She felt him shudder, then his weight was on her, and she wrapped her arms around the dampness of his shoulders, holding his heart against hers. This couldn't be all there was. It couldn't end.

His lips tasted her throat, his breathing ragged in her ears, and as Buck left her, rolling onto his side, she went with him. She settled into the surety of his embrace, closed her eyes and refused to think about tomorrow.

When Steven woke, the cabin was dark and the air cool. His body was satiated, but he knew he would never get enough of Alicia. There was a basic hunger in him that he doubted could ever be satisfied. As she settled against him with a contented sigh, he closed his eyes and just held her. He knew he had to let her go, but not just yet. Not until the roads were cleared. Not until reality made itself known. He held her to his side, relishing the silkiness of her hair against his skin, the way her head rested on his shoulder and her slender hand lay trustingly across his stomach.

For a moment he remembered the first time he'd lain in this bed with her. It had been life and death then, and in a way, it was life and death now. He had life as long as he felt her heat against him, as long as he inhaled the sweetness that clung to her, and as long as he didn't get more than the length of his touch away from her.

She stirred and just the feel of her breasts against his side was enough to make his body tighten. Life was here for him, in every way, and when Alicia was gone, he knew he'd still breathe and move and do what he had to do. But that didn't mean he'd ever feel alive again.

Carefully, he turned to press his lips to her hair. If he could only keep her, if there was a way he could do what he had to do and still have Alicia be with him. He closed his eyes. If there was only a way... There had to be something he could do, some way he could work it out.

"Are you awake?" she whispered.

He felt her words vibrate against him, and the sound surround him. "Uh-huh."

She shifted away from him, the feeling strangely isolating, until she raised herself on her elbow and rested her head on her hand to look at him. The sheet slid down, revealing her bare breasts and the rosy nipples, but she didn't make a move to cover herself. Steven remembered the taste of her, the heaviness of her breasts in his hands. And his body tightened even more.

"Where do you think Pax is?"

The dog. He hadn't thought about him for a very long time. "Out running around now that the snow's stopped, I suppose."

A frown drew a fine line between her incredible eyes. "Do you think—?"

"Absolutely not." The idea of leaving her bed was literally painful for him right now. "He's fine. He'll be back when he wants to come back."

"You're right." She touched her tongue to her pale lips. "I've been thinking."

He brushed at her curls, skimming the tips of his fingers across her forehead. "About the dog?"

"No, about me."

"What about you?"

"The way I was. The real me."

"And what's the real you?"

"Restless, impulsive, too ready to jump in without thinking. It's always been a disaster." She dipped her head and touched her lips to his chest, then drew back, her eyes glowing when they met his. "But not this time. It's crazy and impulsive, but not a disaster at all."

He let his gaze skim over her features, the act a way of memorizing the image in front of him. God, he wanted this memory to last forever. "Are you sure it isn't?"

Her laughter was rough and unsteady. "Oh, I'm sure," she whispered, her hand on his stomach slowly moving on his skin. Her fingers spanned his diaphragm, the touch like fire on him. "I know that when you're ready, you'll tell me what's going on."

He reached up with his free hand and caught a lock of her hair, twining it around his finger. "That can never happen, love, never."

The frown came back, fleetingly. "It can. We've got time."

He knew that time was the one thing they didn't have. He knew as soon as the snowplows came through, she'd have to go. But he couldn't say the words. "We've got right now," he whispered.

She raked her fingers lightly over his chest, the vague abrasiveness of her nails sending shivers through his body. "You know, I've given my sister and foster mother lots of things to worry about. I've really hurt them. I never meant to, but I did." She traced the outline of his nipple with the tip of her finger and it grew hard. "I never will again. I made a promise to Ali before I left for this trip."

"What promise?" he breathed, his voice low and unsteady.

"I told you. That I'd never leave her again. I'd never disappear."

If he did something crazy, like asking her to go with him, to give up everything for a completely new life, she'd leave everything behind. And he knew that she couldn't do that. And it ripped at his heart. "And you'll keep the promise?"

"I want to." She inhaled. "No, I *need* to."

Steven knew what he needed, and knew that he'd only have it for this moment, for this beat of his heart. "Enough talking," he whispered and drew her down to him. His mouth captured hers, and with her heart beating against his, he went to her and he loved her as if it was the last time he'd ever love anyone in his life.

Chapter 12

When Alicia awoke, she felt as if she was coming out of gentleness into a place of deep peace and pleasure. Then she stirred and didn't feel heat against her, or Buck's arms around her. And that peace began to slip away. She opened her eyes to a dull grayness, and she knew it was morning. And Buck wasn't with her anymore.

She looked to her right, but the place he'd lain was empty. The pillow still held the impression of his head, and her body still felt the lingering effects of his lovemaking. She shifted, feeling a tenderness in her breasts, and as she sank back, she knew she was right where she belonged. The place Fate had waiting for her since the beginning of time.

She wanted Buck here with her. She wanted to hold and be held, to love and be loved. That thought made her sigh. Buck hadn't mentioned love during the night, but she'd felt it, in every touch, in every caress, and she knew the admission would come. And she'd love him back. She'd know who he was, and what was going on. And she'd love him for the rest of her life.

She pushed herself up in bed and looked around the room. "Buck?" she called, but there was no answer. She stretched and couldn't see Pax either. Then she noticed the fire was almost out, just a crumbling pile of glowing ashes in the bottom of the grate.

"He must have gone for wood," she murmured to herself. "He'll be back soon." She scrambled out of bed and hurried into the bathroom. While she showered, she thought what she'd do. As soon as the phone was working, she had to call Ali and Lydia. She could explain enough to keep them from worrying, then she'd have to contact Jon. After that, she and Buck could talk and get things straight.

As she stepped out of the shower and began to towel herself, she wondered what she could say to Jon. "Sorry, but it's off, it's all over." She almost laughed. "I found a man who can make every dream I ever had come true." She sobered at the truth of that statement. That was what it was all about. Dreams. And every dream she had now was centered around Buck.

She grabbed the shirt she'd worn the day before and slipped it on. Then she went out into the bedroom. Buck still wasn't there. "I know," she said to herself. "Breakfast."

She hurried into the kitchen and stood in the middle of the room looking around. She was a terrible cook, but she could make toast, and Buck had plenty of peanut butter. She walked over to the refrigerator and saw a piece of paper taped to the front.

She'd never seen a sample of Buck's writing before beyond the signatures on the papers she'd found, but the writing looked like she'd have expected it to. It was large and looping and hard to read. *"Alicia. Road getting cleared. Gone to see if your car can be driven. Back soon."* And no signature.

She smiled. He'd be back soon. She took out the peanut butter, then crossed to get the bread and toast it. "Life is strange," she murmured. "And it's wonderful."

Steven had lain awake while Alicia slept, and when the light of dawn had begun to filter into the cabin, he'd heard the snowplows outside. It had all ended then. He'd stayed in bed holding a sleeping Alicia for as long as he could, but he knew he had to leave. He'd decided to get to her car, see if he could get it running and out of the drift, then bring it back for her.

During the long hike to the car with Pax by his side, he'd tried to stop thinking, to stop a desperate attempt to make sense out of what had happened and come across a way he wouldn't have to give up Alicia. But even before he got to the car and found it effectively stuck, he'd faced the fact that Shaw or his people would always be a threat. There was no way he could have any links to the past. If he made one slipup, Shaw would find him. And if Alicia was with him, she'd be caught in the fallout.

Now, as he turned off the cleared road and started through the snow to the cabin, he felt as if he was going to his own execution. Then he realized that was exactly what he was facing.

He stopped at the porch, feeling Pax brush past him to the door. The dog looked back over his shoulder at Steven, then scratched on the door. "You're out all night, then you want me to be your doorman," Steven said as he went up the stairs.

He hesitated, then grabbed the handle and opened the door. Pax hurried inside while Steven stood in the doorway. He knew what he had to do, he just didn't know how he would go about doing it.

Alicia heard the door open, and before she could go back into the living room, Pax came bounding into the kitchen to her. She dropped down to pat him and hug her arms around his neck, then she looked over the dog's head and saw Buck in the doorway.

He still had on his leather jacket, but it was open, and he was in his stocking feet. The joy in her at seeing him was overwhelming, but when he just watched her, she suddenly felt unsure of herself. How could she love him so much, yet not be capable of getting up and going to him? She patted the dog's back, then got to her feet. "You're back," she said.

He stood in the entry, his hair pulled back in a ponytail, his eyes narrowed. His expression was just as unreadable as it had been the first time she saw him. Something was wrong. All the closeness of the night had dissolved in the day, and it hurt.

"I was making peanut butter and toast for breakfast." She tried to laugh, to lighten the mood. "I'm not much of a cook, but I can make toast." When he didn't say a thing, but just kept watching her, she touched Pax on the head. "Where was Pax?"

"Outside. He showed up early this morning. Your car's stuck completely. I'll drive you to the Welshes' house."

He would have turned and walked away if she hadn't stopped him. "Buck?"

He looked back at her. This was all wrong. It was out of balance, and she had no idea why. "I...I don't want to go there. When the phone's fixed, I'll call."

He looked at her, not talking, not moving, and the silence in the room was a tangible thing. Just when Alicia was ready to scream, to ask him where the man who had held her during the night had gone, a shrill ringing echoed in the cabin.

At first Alicia had no idea what it was, then she realized it was the phone. Without a word, Buck turned and went to answer it. She watched him move across the room, away from her, and she could feel the emotional distance growing with each step he took. She couldn't bear it, and she went after him.

Steven was thankful for the interruption. If he'd had to look at Alicia any longer, standing there in his shirt, her beauty more striking than ever before, he didn't know what he might have done. As he reached for the receiver, he closed his hand over the plastic and pulled it to his ear.

"Rider, a message from Sampson," the man said on the other end.

"Go ahead."

"You have to get out of there. Sampson's on his way. Be ready to go when he gets there."

This put everything into perspective. The choice was taken out of his hands. "I will be," he said and hung up.

He took a breath before he turned to go back in the kitchen. He hadn't heard Alicia move, and he wasn't expecting her to be less than five feet from him, watching him, waiting. "It works," she said.

"Seems to. Why don't you call and let Jon know you're on your way."

She didn't move, and he had to fight the urge to reach out and touch her. Just one more contact, just one, but he knew if he felt her under his hands again, he might never be able to let her go. And that's just what he had to do. He'd never understood love before Alicia, and now he understood a love so deep he preferred to have Alicia safe and away from him, than with him and in danger.

"Buck, we..." She touched her tongue to her lips as she clasped her hands in front of her. He saw her take a deep, shuddering breath before she said, "What's going on?"

He shrugged. "What do you mean?"

"What do I mean?" She exhaled, and color stained her cheeks. "How can you ask what I mean?" Her eyes grew bright, but she didn't cry, thank goodness. "You were here. I...I didn't imagine what happened between us, and now you want to just drive me over to Jon's and drop me off like a bag of groceries."

"I didn't mean it like that." He pushed his hands in his pockets and tried to distance himself from the situation. If he could build some protection, then he could do this. "I just meant, it's time to move on. What happened between us was wonderful, but that's all it can be. I told you I've got a life that's complicated. And I explained that last night was last night. It couldn't be any more."

"But things have changed," she said, taking a step closer to him. "We can work it out."

"No, we can't. I need to do what I have to do, and you need to get on with your own life."

"Just like that? Thanks, but no thanks?"

"I told you this was what we had, this place, this time. There can't be any more."

She came even closer and he steeled himself. "Why?"

"You told me last night about your promise to Ali. Well, I've made a promise and I can't break it."

"And that means that we can't—"

"It means that I have to go and you can't come with me."

"Buck, I..." She bit her lip and the tears were very real now and precariously close to falling. "I love you."

He heard the words, but he couldn't let them settle into his soul. Not when his need to tell her that she was loved more than life itself almost choked him. "You can't love me."

She came even closer, then her hands touched his chest. His breathing all but stopped, and he clenched his hands in his pockets so tightly that he felt his nails digging into his palms. "But I do love you."

The tears slipped down her cheeks, and he felt literally sick at what he was doing. Words he'd have given anything to hear before this mess were now like a death sentence to him. He pushed his hands behind his back, literally forcing himself not to touch her and stop those tears. "Don't love me, Alicia," he said, his voice flat in his own ears. "I'm not worth it. You've got a whole life ahead of you. And it doesn't include me."

She didn't move or speak for what seemed like an eternity, then everything shifted. The tears were still there, bright and damp on her lashes, but he could see her jaw set. She swiped at her eyes, the motion sharp and angry. Color touched her paleness and she shook her head. "All right. You don't have to say anything else. I'll walk to Jon's." She wiped a shaky hand over her face again. "I know when I'm not wanted."

Not wanted? If she only knew how very much she was wanted, how much she'd be wanted for the rest of his life. "No, you won't. I'll drive you. Just give me time to get the Jeep out and—"

Alicia wasn't about to cry and throw herself at Buck's feet, begging him to let her stay and not send her away. This wasn't some foster home where she'd always been the odd man out, where she hadn't belonged and got moved around at the whim of Social Services or the foster family. She hadn't begged then, and she wouldn't start now.

No matter how much it hurt, or how wrong she'd been last night, she was getting out of here. She had jumped in with both feet, acting impulsively once again, and once again it had become an unmitigated disaster. Bad choices seemed to be her specialty. But this was worse than anything she'd ever done before, down to and including her fiasco with Mick Terrine.

She turned from the sight of the silent, painfully remote Buck and hurried into the bedroom. She found the clothes she'd discarded last night and she blocked the memories of how they had been taken off her. Memories had no place in her mind now, not when she was just barely holding herself together.

"Don't remember," she muttered to herself as she headed for the bathroom. Once in the small room, she slammed the door shut, and the fear that she'd explode and scatter into a million pieces kept her from moving for what could have been minutes or hours. Then from somewhere a numbness appeared and fell around her like a protective cloak.

By rote she dressed in her own clothes, then dropped his shirt on the sink and turned. Her image in the mirror couldn't have been more foreign to her than if it had been a stranger looking back at her. She looked stunned, like a deer who had been caught in the headlights of an oncoming car. And she knew if she didn't get out of here right now, she'd be struck by that car. She pressed her hands on the sides of the sink and leaned toward her reflection. "You damn fool," she ground out through clenched teeth. "You've never gone this far before. Never."

Then she realized something—this was the first mistake in her life that didn't affect anyone but herself. She was the one who had the pain, and she was the one who would have to figure out what to do about it. She quickly turned on the water, cupped it in both her hands, then splashed it on her face. Looking back at her reflection, she saw water dripping off her lashes and trickling down her face. Her hair was dark where it was wet, and it curled against her skin.

"And I'll get through this," she whispered. "I'll get through it, and I won't hurt anyone else because of it."

This pain was all hers. Alone. Not even Ali could share this. She wiped her face with a towel, then raked her fingers through her hair to brush it back from her face. "All alone," she breathed, the words echoing around her, then turned and went out of the room.

Buck was by the windows looking out, and she crossed to get her jacket. She didn't look at Buck while she slipped on the garment, then pushed her feet into her boots. She felt in her pocket for her wallet and the rental keys, then turned to open the door and escape. But Buck was at the door before she could get out, and she jerked her hand back, terrified that he'd touch her. She didn't know what she'd do if she felt his hand on her again.

"I'll drive you anywhere you want to go," he said, no more than a foot from her.

She stared at the floor. "I don't need you to drive me. I can walk."

"I said I'll drive you."

She made herself look at him, thankful the numbness was still intact and thankful she was facing a stranger. There wasn't a trace of the man she'd loved last night in this man so close to her. His face was expressionless, his eyes cold and closed. Her legs didn't feel at all steady, and she found herself agreeing. "All right."

Without another word, he reached around her and opened the door. Pax hurried after him and followed him out onto the porch. Alicia took one last look around the cabin, realizing there wasn't a hint that she'd even been there. She left nothing behind and took nothing with her.

She stepped out into the cold bright day, and she was surprised that the driveway had been cleared, exposing the half circle that ran from the road up to the porch, then curved back to the road. Snow had been pushed to the sides, piled into drifts that were almost five feet in height.

Alicia saw Buck heading for the garage with the dog by his side. The clear light of the sun glinted off his raven hair, and he moved easily, his strides long and fluid. A man who didn't need anyone, least of all her. She hugged her arms around herself and looked away. He was alone by choice. She was alone because she didn't have a choice.

The sound of a motor drew her attention and she turned to see a red Jeep backing out of the garage and into the cleared drive. She stepped down onto the driveway, and the Jeep came toward her, then stopped right in front of her. She pulled the passenger door open and got inside. Pax was in the back, his chin resting on the back of the seat, and she could feel the numbness slip just enough for her to feel a deep sadness for the dog she wouldn't see again.

She glanced at Buck, but he was holding the steering wheel, staring straight ahead. "Close the door," he said.

She restrained herself from slamming it, then settled back in the seat. Buck drove around the drive and out onto the road, heading in the opposite direction Alicia had been going the night of the storm. The silence in the Jeep wasn't broken until they drove across the main highway and started up a short hill. As they crested it, Alicia saw a house on the left set back from the road. She didn't need to see the discreet sign by huge iron gates that read "Welsh" to know where she was.

Buck stopped the truck at the closed gates and rolled down his window. He pushed the button of an intercom set into the columns and waited. "Yes?" some-one said from inside.

"Miss Alicia Sullivan."

"Come right up," the voice said, and the gates slowly swung open.

Buck drove the Jeep through the opening and started up the drive that had been cleared to expose cobbled bricks set in a herringbone pattern. Alicia looked straight ahead at a house that was as pretentious as the cabin was simple. The two-story structure was done in natural wood and rock, with numerous chimneys releasing smoke from wood fires into the still air. At the end of the driveway, a wooden rail edged a dozen broad steps that led up to an entry sheltered by a crescent-shaped covering.

"Here you are," Buck said as he stopped the Jeep and let the motor idle.

She didn't want to look at him, but she found herself able to meet his gaze and utter polite words. "Thank you for all you did for me."

He watched her from under lowered lids but didn't speak.

She reached behind her and touched Pax on his head. "Take care of Pax," she managed, then swallowed hard as she gripped the door handle tightly. "Buck, I—" She bit her lip and scrambled out of the Jeep.

As she turned to close the door, she met Buck's gaze. For a moment, she felt the impact of his blue eyes, an intensity in their depths that she didn't understand, and she held to the door for support. "Goodbye, Buck," she whispered.

"Steven Rider," he said abruptly.

"What?"

"I'm Steven Rider," he said, then drove off, the door slipping out of her hand and swinging shut as the Jeep headed for the gates.

"Steven Rider," she said softly. A name. His name. But why did he tell her now? Why would he tell her at all?

"Alicia!" She heard her name called, and she slowly turned away from the sight of the Jeep going through the gates. The numbness was dissolving at an alarming rate and all because he'd told her his name.

She saw Jon at the top of the steps by open double doors, but she couldn't focus on him. Steven Rider. It wasn't until Jon was running down the steps toward her that she finally saw him clearly. His blond hair, short and styled, his broad face, all smiles, and leather pants along with a brown cable-knit pullover, defining his solid build.

Alicia didn't have time to say or do anything before Jon scooped her up into his arms, his hold solid and sure. And she found herself holding on to him, burying her face in the wool of his sweater until she could almost believe it was Buck holding her. That this was Buck who wanted her and would never let her go.

"Alicia. I've missed you," Jon whispered, and the sound of his voice brought reality back to her with a thud. It was over. And Buck hadn't made any promises. It had been her hopes, her dreams that had been smashed.

Suddenly Jon's hold on her was suffocating. She eased back, until Jon's hands rested on her shoulders, almost a duplicate of the way Buck had held her last night. She looked at Jon and had to swallow hard repeatedly to control a sudden rush of sickness that burned the back of her throat and had nothing to do with Jon.

She didn't love Jon. She never had. She loved a man who had just disappeared from her life. Jon leaned toward her and kissed her. The contact was cold and shocking. As he stood back and smiled at her, he said, "I knew you'd hole up in Gibson. Personally, I think it's a nice place to wait out a storm, but I'm glad you're here now." He looked past her. "Where's your car and your luggage?"

He thought she'd been in Gibson all this time, and that was fine with her. She certainly didn't want him to know anything about Buck, or Joe Riley, or Steven Rider. Whoever he was. She didn't want anyone to know about Buck or her time there. "I got stuck in a snowbank back down the road."

"Then how did you get here?"

"A man . . . he came by. The car's stuck and it's out of gas. I left my suitcase in it."

"Is the car close by?"

"On the other side of the main road. I turned the wrong way. I'm not good at driving in this sort of weather, and I was just thankful the man found me. He gave me a ride."

"Who was he?" Jon asked.

"I don't know," she said truthfully, his hands getting heavy on her shoulders. She had names, but she didn't know who he was.

"Too bad," Jon murmured and switched to take her by the arm and go with her up the stairs. "I would have loved to thank him for being such a good Samaritan."

"He didn't want thanks," she said as they went up the steps.

"I've been telling my parents all about you, and they're dying to finally meet you."

Her heart lurched sickeningly. "What did you tell them?"

"Don't worry, I didn't tell them about your past. Just that you're a terrific person and I wanted you here to meet them."

Her past? That hadn't even come to her mind. "What did you tell them—that I hatched six months ago?"

He laughed, not realizing that she was getting mad. "Of course not. Just that you're an orphan and travel agent."

"A helper, not an agent."

"Whatever," he said breezily. "I told them that I'm crazy about you. They were anxious to meet you, to get to know you, but they had to go into Gibson to get some things for the party tonight."

A party. New Year's Eve. She didn't know what she'd expected to do once she got here, but it wasn't to party and pretend that life was normal. She knew at that moment that she couldn't stay any longer than it took to explain things to Jon. But she needed a car. "What about my car?"

An older man in heavy outside clothes came out the door and looked down at Jon and Alicia. Jon stopped on a lower step. "Lawrence, I was just going to ring for you."

"Yes, sir. What can I do for you?"

"There's a car down the road a ways stuck in the snow and out of gas. Get over there with the Land

Rover and some gas. Then bring it back here as soon as you can."

Alicia fished in her pocket and took out the keys, holding them out to the man. "Here are the keys."

The man came down the steps, took the keys and kept going. "I'll be back as quickly as possible, sir," he said.

Jon led the way up to massive double doors, and he pushed back the door that Lawrence had left partially ajar and let her precede him into his home. Alicia stepped into a foyer that filled both stories, with planked walls that blended into a vaulted ceiling, a black-and-white marble floor, and a staircase to the right that led up to a second-floor balcony.

Jon called out to a small woman in a stiff black dress who was hurrying down the stairs. "Hannah, get Miss Sullivan's room ready."

"Yes, sir," she said and was about to go back up the stairs.

"Jon, don't bother," Alicia heard herself saying.

The woman paused, and Jon turned to Alicia. "Excuse me?"

She felt overheated and claustrophobic now that she was inside. This was going to be even harder than she'd first thought. "We need to talk, Jon."

He waved a hand at the maid, and the woman hurried back upstairs. Then Jon faced Alicia. "We can talk later. We've got time."

"No, we don't."

His expression tightened and lost any hint of pleasure. "What's going on?"

"Can't we talk someplace more private?"

"This is fine. What's the problem?"

She looked at him and hated herself. But she couldn't let this go any further. "I can't marry you."

He put up both hands out toward her. "Just a minute. Just a minute. You just got here, walked in and it's over, just like that?"

"No, not just like that." It felt as if she hadn't seen Jon for an eternity, and that it had taken that eternity for her to figure out her life. "I just can't get married. I'm not ready."

"Not ready?"

"Jon, I—"

"Not ready?" he said a bit more loudly.

So much for the dream of telling him, having him understand, and her walking away. Anger brought a flush to his face. "I'm sorry," she said.

"You're sorry?"

"Don't do this."

"Do what?" he demanded.

"I'm trying to explain, to tell you that I'm not ready for marriage, that I might never be."

"And this all came to you in Gibson, or did it come to you when you were in L.A. and you just had to fly out to tell me in person?"

Alicia was beginning to feel her own tinge of anger. This was a horrible situation, but she would have never guessed that Jon would make it even worse. "No, it's just that I've been thinking a lot about it. I told you I needed time to sort things out. And I realized—"

"You aren't ready."

"Jon, I'm being honest with you."

"It's about time," he muttered.

"What does that mean?"

"Actually, I've been thinking a lot myself. When I asked you to marry me, I wondered if a person can really change, if she can go from crazy to sane, or from reckless to cautious?"

"Jon, I—"

He cut her off. "Do you believe in transformations? Your sister doesn't."

She blinked at that. "My sister? What does she have to do with this?"

"She called. The first phone call that got through this morning was from her. She's been worried about you, and when I told her you hadn't arrived yet, she sounded upset."

"She's worried. I knew she would be." She didn't want Ali to have any part in this fiasco. She needed to call, to explain and smooth things over. "I need to use your phone to call her."

"She was worried about your welfare, Alicia, but I think part of her was almost as worried that you'd reverted to type, that you'd taken off. It seems that you run away at the drop of a hat. That you can't face commitment or responsibility. You get angry and take off."

"My sister wouldn't have ever said anything like that to you. You're making this up."

"She didn't use those very words, but the meaning was there." Jon came a step closer. "She was right, wasn't she?"

She could barely draw air into her lungs. "No, she wasn't. And neither are you."

"I know you, Alicia, and I—"

Suddenly anger exploded in her. "You know me? I don't think you do at all. Do you know that I talk to myself, that I can make one hell of a snowball, and I can make snow angels?"

He looked at her as if she'd lost her mind. "Snow angels?"

"Snow angels," she muttered. "You don't know me, Jon. You never knew the real me, and I never knew the real you."

He paled at her words, but didn't move. "Who is the real you?"

"Not the woman you asked to marry you." And not the woman who let Buck drive away. She'd never been weak and submissive, and she knew right then that she wasn't going to be pushed again. Not by Jon, and not by Buck. She was going back to the cabin, and she was going to talk to Buck, to tell him that no matter what trouble he was in, she'd be with him. Heaven knew she'd been in enough trouble of her own. And it was a lot easier if there were two against the world rather than one.

Chapter 13

Alicia couldn't believe how simple things were. She was going to be with Buck, no matter what, and she would never look back with regret on it.

"I asked a woman, who I thought had reformed, to marry me," Jon was saying, his jaw set, his eyes filled with anger.

"Reformed?" That word hit her hard. She was Alicia, and heaven help her, she wasn't about to change. The only thing she'd never do again was run away. "You make me sound like a criminal. I'm not. I'm just a fool," she said. "And I was trying to be what you wanted, what everyone wanted. And I can't be. I'm what I am, who I am, and I can't marry you."

"Alicia—?"

"I'll wait until Lawrence brings the car, then I have to leave." She looked around. She was going to call Buck. "Now, can I use your phone?"

He moved to one side and motioned to an antique breakfront on the far side of the foyer. "Do whatever you want," Jon muttered. "I'm sure you will, anyway."

Despite the bitter words, she felt as if a horrible burden had been lifted off her shoulders. It was a relief to put an end to something that should never have started. From now on, she was who she was, who she wanted to be. Not what others thought she should be. And she'd do what she knew she had to do.

She reached for the phone, then realized that she didn't have any idea what the phone number at the cabin was. That was all right. She wouldn't call. She didn't want to give Buck time to build walls before she could even get there.

Alicia dialed Ali's number in Los Angeles and it only rang once before it was answered. "Hello?"

"Ali, it's me."

"Oh, thank goodness, Alicia. Are you alright? Where are you?"

"I'm fine. I'm at Jon's."

"Jon's?" She sounded legitimately surprised. "I sort of thought that..."

"That if I wasn't frozen to death, I ran away?"

"I never said that."

"It's all right. You've got every right to think that. The idea of running away is pretty appealing right now."

"You wouldn't—"

"No, I wouldn't. I'm not running away anymore. I'm going to straighten out my life, then I'm coming home."

"It's over with Jon, isn't it?" Ali asked softly.

"You don't sound surprised."

"I'm not. I wish it could have been what you wanted, but I had a gut instinct that it wouldn't be."

"It wasn't. But I know what I want now. How are you feeling?"

"Very pregnant. And very bad for you."

"Don't feel bad for me, Ali. I've finally come to my senses."

"I thought you were getting pretty sensible."

"Finally." She heard a car outside. "I'll call to let you know when I'm coming back. I have to go now, but I love you," she said and hung up.

Steven drove slowly on the way back, even though he knew Sampson would probably be there waiting, anxious to get going. He flexed his hands on the steering wheel and wondered why he'd told Alicia his name. It didn't make sense and it could even be dangerous. But he'd done it.

He shook his head sharply to try to clear his thoughts. Nothing made sense anymore. Not a thing. His future sure as hell didn't. He slowed as he neared the cabin and wasn't surprised to see tire prints over the ones the Jeep had made on the way out. Sampson was here. He pulled onto the driveway, but didn't see a car in front of the house. Then he noticed the garage door was down. Sampson must have parked in there to keep out of sight.

Steven drove to the porch steps, and as he touched the key to turn off the engine, he hesitated. He'd never been a man to dream of doing the impossible. Surviving had always been enough for him, but now he wanted more. And he had to fight the idea of going back for Alicia, the idea that if he ran with her and ran long enough and hard enough, they would survive . . . together.

But sanity stopped him from doing it. Wishing it wouldn't make it so. Dreaming it would only make everything turn into a nightmare. He flicked off the motor, pushed the key into his pocket, then got out. The dog jumped to the ground, and they headed for the porch. He took the steps in one stride and reached for the door. He was ready to get on with things, to stop thinking about "what ifs" and dealing with solid fact. Put Shaw away, get a new identity, and make the best of what he had.

He turned the knob, opened the door and stepped inside. "Sorry I wasn't here to greet you," Steven said as he swung the door shut and turned. "But I'm ready . . ."

His voice trailed when he saw a stranger standing by the hearth. Tall and pale in a black overcoat, the man was staring at Steven with a gun in his hand.

"Hello, Rider," the man said.

"He sent you, didn't he?" Steven asked, knowing that the best thing he had ever done in his life was to make Alicia leave.

"It's a job. That's all. You're messing up the man's life, and you have to be stopped."

"It's that cut-and-dried to you?"

"As I said, it's a job."

"If you got a better offer—?"

"I'm not negotiating," he said abruptly, then motioned with the gun for Steven to move away from the partially open door. "Let's make this as simple as possible."

Steven looked at the man, but didn't move. "You said it's a job, so work for your money."

He shrugged. "Have it your way."

Steven braced himself, ready to dive to one side and get as close to the dresser and his gun as he could. But before he could act, the door flew open, Pax ran into the cabin, and as Jaimie L. jerked the gun toward the door, Steven dove right at him. A gunshot rang out, then silence fell on the cabin.

Alicia had never been so nervous in her life. As she left Jon's and headed toward Buck's, she went over and over what she was going to say when she saw Buck again.

"I love you. I'll be with you, no matter what," she said out loud, practicing the sound of the words. "No matter what's wrong, I'll help. I'm good at getting out of trouble." She gripped the steering wheel and slowed as she approached the main highway. "Whoever Shaw is, whatever you did to him, we'll get through it."

She exhaled. "Two people are better than one when there's trouble." And she wasn't going to let Buck send her away, no matter what. She pressed the accelerator and crossed the highway onto the road that led to the cabin. "I'm not going," she'd say, making her voice firm. "I'm staying, Buck. I'm not leaving you."

Buck Jones. Joe Riley. Steven Rider. "He's right. A name doesn't mean a thing. It's the person that counts."

Whether Buck wanted to see her or not, she had a need in her to see him that bordered on a physical hunger. And she knew he cared. He couldn't have been with her last night, touching her, caressing her, loving her, unless he felt something for her. No one was that good an actor.

She saw the cabin to the right, and she pulled between buried pillars that marked the opening to the driveway. She'd only been at the cabin for a few days, but as she approached it, she almost felt as if she were coming home. That feeling had been so fleeting and far between in her life, that it made her heart catch. If she had had any doubt about coming back, it was completely gone now.

She stopped the car at the foot of the porch steps, took a moment to get herself steady, then got out, circled the front and went up the steps. She got to the door, raised her hand to knock, then thought better of it. She wasn't going to give him any warning at all.

She turned the knob, pushed open the door and called out, "Buck, I'm back."

She stepped into the house, and the first thing she noticed was the chill in the air. One glance at the fireplace and she could see the fire was completely out. "Buck?" She looked around and was struck by the perfect order of the room. Not a thing was out of place.

Then she realized it wasn't perfect order, it was emptiness. Everything that had meant Buck was here was gone. No jacket on the peg, no boots on the floor, no books on the desk. She moved farther into the room. The bed had been stripped and the blankets folded at the foot.

"I should never have left," she breathed as she wandered around the cabin, knowing that Buck was gone. "Never, never."

The bathroom was empty, the towels neatly folded. In the kitchen there wasn't a dish out of place. Nothing was on the stove. She opened the cupboard under the sink. Even the garbage was gone. She slammed the door and went back into the living room. She'd never felt so alone in her life.

She froze when she heard a noise on the porch, and she ran to the door and pulled it open. Pax pushed into the cabin, looked at Alicia as if he wasn't at all surprised to see her there. He pressed against her leg, almost the way a cat would, then sank down in his usual place.

He'd left the dog. For some reason she'd thought Buck would take Pax. But he'd left him behind, too. With angry tears in her eyes, she crossed to the wood cabinet, took out some logs and began to methodically rebuild the fire. When the wood caught, Alicia moved back and sat on the couch.

No matter where she looked, she couldn't find a thing of Buck's. It was as if he had never been there, as if nothing had happened there. She pressed her hand flat on the cushion, and the tip of her finger touched something in the space between the two cushions. She tugged and pulled out a dark blue button, a button from one of Buck's shirts. She stared at it on the palm of her hand, then slowly closed her fingers around the plastic. Something solid, something real. Buck had been here. She had proof. The plastic all but cut into her hand as she clenched it in a death grip. She'd loved him.

Tears slipped from her eyes, silently rolling down her cheek, but she didn't pay any attention to them. She couldn't go back to L.A. just yet, and it seemed as natural as breathing to decide to stay right here. She came back; maybe Buck would. Maybe he'd walk in that door and smile and hold out his arms to her. Maybe he'd realize that he loved her as much as she loved him.

The dog stood and came to the couch to drop down by Alicia and settle his muzzle on her thigh. His dark eyes rolled up at her. Alicia stroked his head. "He left both of us, didn't he, Pax?" she murmured.

She reached for the phone, heard the tone, and dialed Ali's number. "Ali?" she said when her sister answered.

"Alicia? Is something wrong?"

She closed her eyes as she kept stroking the dog's head with her free hand. Everything was wrong. "No," she lied. "I've decided to stay in Colorado for a few days. I just wanted you to know."

"But it's New Year's Eve. I was hoping you'd be here to celebrate with us."

"Afraid not. I'm going to take a break. I need to think about things."

"Are you reconsidering Jon's proposal?"

"No, that's over. I need to figure out what I'm going to do with my life."

"Where are you now?"

"Just outside Gibson." She looked at the phone front and read off the phone number. "Call me here if you need me for anything. Tell Lydia and Jack that I wish them a Happy New Year, all right?"

"Sure. Alicia?"

"Yes?"

"Don't be gone too long."

She stared at the fire in the hearth. "I'll call and let you know when I'm flying back."

"What if Jon calls?"

"Tell him to have a happy life," Alicia said. Then she told Ali "Goodbye," and hung up.

She put the phone back, sank into the cushions and closed her eyes. "Happy New Year, Alicia," she breathed, and held tightly to the button in her hand.

Alicia stayed at the cabin with Pax, not willing to give up the slim hope that Buck might come back. But when a dreary New Year's came and went, with three days passing and no word, Alicia knew it was time to go. She didn't give up easily, but she knew when there was no hope left. And the cabin had grown more and more empty as the time passed. It was no longer a healing place, just a place of painful memories.

On the fourth day she'd come to two decisions. She was taking Pax with her, and she was going to drive back to L.A.

She found Pax out on the porch, and after she'd closed the door, she turned to the dog. "So, do you want to come and see Los Angeles?"

Without hesitation, the dog went down the steps and crossed to the car in the drive. "You are psychic," she murmured as she hurried down to the car to open the passenger door for Pax. "I knew you were special the first time I saw you."

While he settled on the front seat, Alicia got behind the wheel and started the car. She took one last look at the cabin, then at the button she had in her hand. She knew the truth of one thing she'd told Buck. She would never regret the time she spent with him here or anything that happened before he disappeared.

She put the button in her pocket, then drove away from the cabin. When she got to Gibson, she stopped at a florist and sent a bouquet to Jon's parents with an apology. Then she bought some groceries and headed west. When darkness came, she found a small motel in southern Utah and stopped for the night. After little sleep, she started out again at dawn.

By noon she felt anxious to get home; she wanted to see Ali and Lydia and Jack. Just outside of Las Vegas, she spotted a small diner and parked in the black-topped parking lot near the front of the flat-roofed building under a spreading shade tree. She could call Ali and get some food, then head straight for Los Angeles.

She left Pax sleeping in the car, put the windows down partway, then went inside the restaurant, into a long room filled with green tables, plastic chairs, a counter that ran along the wall to her left, and garish neon beer signs circling the walls near the ceiling. A low hum of voices mingled with the constant chatter of a sportscaster on a television that had been hung in the corner so it could be viewed from the counter or the booths.

"Booth or table, miss, or do you want to sit at the counter?" someone asked, and Alicia turned to see a waitress standing by the cash register by the door. The heavyset woman was all in green, and Alicia couldn't help but think that she blended into the room perfectly.

"The counter's fine. I need to use a phone."

"They're back there by the rest rooms," she said, pointing. "Do you want some coffee?"

"Yes, please," Alicia said, then headed to the back of the room.

Alicia found the phone in a cubbyhole by the ladies' room and put a call through to Ali's home. When Lydia answered, she knew how much she missed everyone. "Lydia? Is that you?"

"Oh, Alicia. We didn't have any idea how to get ahold of you. The number you gave us just rang and rang. And when I called Jon, he acted as if you were the plague. He isn't a terribly nice person, I don't think. Really quite rude."

"Lydia, Jon's in my past. Don't let him bother you. I just called to let you know I'm on my way home."

"What flight are you coming in on?"

"I'm driving. I'm about two hundred and seventy-five miles away. Can I talk to Ali?"

"Oh, dear, that's why I'm here. Jack just took Ali to the hospital. She went into labor early. I stayed here to try and get ahold of you."

"She's in labor?"

"Just starting, dear. If I'm any judge, you've got time to get here, if you don't dawdle. She's at the main hospital."

"I'm on my way," Alicia said. "I'll meet you there as soon as I can."

"You drive carefully, you hear? I don't want any accidents."

"I'll be careful."

"And wear your seat belt."

"Lydia, tell Ali I'll be there when the baby's born, and I'll be in one piece."

She hung up and went back to the counter. The waitress was just setting a mug of coffee on the counter. "Excuse me," Alicia said. "Can I have another cup to go?"

"Sure, no problem. Anything else?"

"And two roast beef sandwiches to go? One with nothing but the meat and bread, the other with tomatoes, lettuce and mustard? And I'm in a real hurry."

"It won't take five minutes, honey," the waitress said.

Alicia slipped onto the stool nearest the door and took a sip of the strong coffee. The baby was coming early! She felt nervous, anxious to get on the road again and she glanced out the window at her car. Pax wasn't stirring. As she fiddled with a small saltshaker on the counter, she glanced at the television. The news was on, something about demonstrations by workers in Las Vegas, then the screen changed.

The words *"News Update"* flashed across the screen, then a newscaster was talking. *"A major update on the Bryce Sanbourn trial. The news has just been released that one of the key witnesses in the government's case against Sanbourn, Steven Rider, was fatally injured in a single-car accident in a Virginia suburb last night."*

Alicia heard "Steven Rider" and the coffee cup stopped at her lips. The name, it could be anyone. It's just a name. Then a picture flashed on the screen, the same picture that had been laminated on the ID cards at the cabin.

"An unidentified passenger in the car was also killed. Moses Kaufman, the prosecutor in the case, refused to be interviewed, but Rider's death isn't thought to affect the strength of the case. He had finished his

testimony about his discovery that Sanbourn was using the alias Clarence Shaw in the Houston area. Shaw had been...."

"Honey, you all right? You look as if you've just lost your best friend."

Alicia looked at the waitress who was leaning toward her across the counter. She couldn't focus. The whole world felt blurred and unreal. Steven Rider was dead. He'd testified against Shaw. Everything fit into place for Alicia at the same time the word "dead" hit her in the middle.

Gone. Buck. Dead. She felt the coffee cup slip from her fingers and watched the brown liquid splash on the counter and spray across the front of the waitress' uniform. He couldn't be dead. He couldn't have stopped existing. She would have known. She would have felt it.

The waitress was sopping up coffee with towels, muttering to herself and casting Alicia dark looks. But Alicia couldn't hear anything over the echoes of the newscaster's words that still rang in her mind. *"Steven Rider was fatally injured in a single-car accident."*

And Ali was giving birth to a new life. Cycles. Life went on. Alicia fumbled in her purse for money, dropped it on the counter, then shocked herself by being able to stand and walk. The waitress caught up to her at the door and pushed a bag into her hands. Her lips moved, but Alicia had no idea what she was saying.

All she knew was that she had to get back to Los Angeles.

Chapter 14

Six months later

Alicia had most of her packing done by the time Ali got to the house and called out from near the front door, "Alicia? Where are you?"

"In the bedroom."

As she put her swim suit and coverup in the suitcase, she heard Alicia coming down the hall. "It didn't take you long to get over here," she said as she snapped the lid shut on the suitcase and turned.

Ali was in the doorway, her hair pulled back in a high ponytail, her face free of makeup, and the baby in a carrying sling, lying snugly against her breasts. Only the suggestion of pale blond fuzz could be seen over the blue cotton of the sling. Ali looked like a teenager in shorts and tank top, her figure back to normal and the only traces of the pregnancy were fuller breasts from breast-feeding Taylor Anne.

"What's going on?" Ali asked as she picked her way past the discarded clothes Alicia had tossed into piles on the floor. "Are you going someplace?"

Alicia lifted the suitcase, set it on the floor, then she dropped down on the bed and looked up at her sister. "I'm going to Mexico, Ali."

"Mexico?"

"Remember that cabin we went to when Harry was alive?"

"Sure, the one just below Rosarita Beach." She smiled a bit wistfully. "It was great. The best summer I ever had."

"The strangest thing happened. I was on the computer yesterday at the agency and it came up as available for the Fourth of July weekend. So I rented it."

Ali smiled with what could have been relief. "Thank goodness."

"Thank goodness for what?"

"You're finally doing something for fun." She patted the baby's back softly as she spoke. "We were beginning to think that your body had been taken over by a boring alien. You've done nothing but work, help with Taylor or sit in here since that fiasco in Colorado. I didn't think that the breakup with Jon would have hit you so hard."

"It didn't," she said quickly. Jon was such a faint memory that she'd be hard put to even remember what he looked like. The nightmares, the moments of disorientation when she woke to complete loneliness and a dull ache behind her breastbone had nothing to do with Jon at all. "I've been trying to get my life in order."

"I never thought I'd say this, but I was just about ready to tell you I wanted the old Alicia back—the crazy, impetuous one."

That shocked her. "You're kidding?"

"No, I'm not." When the baby began to fuss, Ali took her out of the sling, tossed the cotton holder on the bed and sat the baby on her knees. "We wanted the real Aunt Alicia to come back, didn't we, Taylor Anne?"

Alicia looked at her niece, at the chubby face, the clear blue eyes, the suggestion of hair that would be the color of her father's, and the hint of a dimple on her left cheek. Taylor Anne had been premature, but had quickly made up for it. Ali looked as if she had been a mother all her life. She held the baby with ease, loving her, caring for her. And Alicia felt a twinge of jealousy. Ali really did have it all. A happy life, Jack, the baby and a free-lance photography business. She had everything.

Alicia touched the baby's hand and the tiny fingers closed around hers. "Taylor Anne wants a sane, sensible aunt who's got control of her life, don't you, Taylor?"

"She wants the real you, no matter who that is."

Alicia looked at Ali. "The real me? I don't even know who that is anymore. I wonder if I ever did."

Ali frowned as she bounced the baby up and down on her knee. "What's wrong? What happened in Colorado if it wasn't Jon?"

She stood. "I had a sort of self-realization thing, I guess. I figured out that I was trying to live the way everyone wanted me to live, the way Jon wanted his wife to be, the way I thought you and Lydia wanted me to live so I didn't give you any grief. And I lost myself somewhere along the way. Then I thought I found the person I was meant to be, but it turned out I lost even more.''

She could remember Buck without tears now, without that inability to function, but it still hurt deep in her soul. She stooped and kissed the top of the baby's silky head. ''I need to go away for a while, just a week or so, and when I get back, I'll be back to normal. Whatever that is.''

Ali grabbed Alicia's hand. ''Promise you'll be back?''

''Yes, I promise. Although why you want me, I'll never figure that out.''

''I love you. You're my family, my sister.''

''You've got a great family. The baby and Jack, and Lydia's positively blossomed since you've made this wonderful life for yourself.''

''You sure haven't,'' Ali murmured.

''I told you, I'll try to blossom when I get back.'' She glanced at the clock by the bed. ''I need to get going.''

''Do you want me to drive you to the airport?''

''No, I'm driving so Pax can come with me.''

Ali looked around the room. ''Where is the beast?''

''Eating out back. Tanking up before the long trek. Do me a favor and tell Lydia I'll call when I get there. She had to go and take Mrs. Ramsey, the neighbor, to the doctor's. Tell Jack I wished him a happy Fourth of July.''

''You can tell him yourself,'' Ali said, looking past Alicia to the door.

Alicia turned and saw Jack in the entry, his usual suit coat and tie gone in favor of a faded Hawaiian shirt, jeans and scuffed running shoes.

"You're taking off?" he asked as he made his way across the room and reached out for Taylor Anne.

"Just for a week. I'm going to Mexico. I got a deal on a cottage just below Rosarita Beach."

Jack held the baby as if he'd been doing it all his life, and when Taylor Anne grabbed at his sandy blond hair, he ignored her tugs. "Ali told me about that area. Too bad we couldn't come along and make it a family vacation, but I've got a lot of work to do, even over the holiday."

Alicia patted the baby's diapered bottom, then turned and lifted her suitcase. "Work, be happy, and Pax and I will be thinking about you when the fireworks go off."

Alicia arrived at the cottage just before sunset. She drove her white convertible with the top down along the silvery expanse of private beach, balmy air stirring her hair. Pax sat on the seat by her, his head lifted as if he were testing the air touched with the tanginess of the nearby ocean.

She spotted the cottage near the dunes and drove toward it, up to the front steps that led to a wraparound porch and the entry. She had barely stopped and turned off the engine, before Pax jumped over the side and left her to sit there, looking at the cottage.

Realistically, she'd known it would have aged. It was, but she hadn't expected it to look so shabby. The siding was warped and silvered from age and the elements. The roof pitched high in the middle and had been covered with pale blue tiles that were curling at the edges. The multipaned windows and doors that opened to the outside had been trimmed in a pale pink paint that looked oxidized. Even the sun, reflecting back the gold in the panes of glass, couldn't quite make it look magical.

"So, that's what I expected? Magic?" But it was just a house, a tiny cottage that many people had rented over the years. No magic here. And she doubted there was any left in the world. In that moment she almost called Pax back from where he was running on the beach toward the water. Her impulse was to leave, but she stopped herself.

"Enough running away," she told herself. She'd committed herself to stay here for a week, and she'd stay. She'd go for walks, swim, lie in the sun, and maybe something *magical* would happen. Maybe she could go back to Los Angeles and not think about Buck at all.

For the two days before the Fourth of July, she wandered the private beach, lay out in the baking heat of the sun and slept fitfully at night. Dreams haunted her, the same dreams she'd had ever since she'd watched the television and heard about Buck being killed. Strange, she couldn't think of Buck as Steven Rider. It was Buck she saw in her dreams, Buck smiling at her, Buck reaching out for her, and Buck who wasn't there when she reached out for him.

Late in the afternoon of the Fourth, Alicia dressed in brief white shorts, a pink halter top and went barefoot out onto the beach. Pax ran at her side down to the water, and they followed the waterline to the south. When she'd rented the cottage, the agent had told her there would firework displays both north and south, and they could be seen from the cottage area.

She thought she'd go south to a clump of rocks raised above the tide line and sit there to see the display. As she walked, the sand was warm on her bare feet, and a gentle breeze from the west skimmed over the ocean, rippling its peacefulness with small waves. When she reached the rocks, she sat on the warm granite and looked around.

She saw Pax, circling and making lunges at sea gulls, scattering the birds, then running after them to the water's edge to bark as they took flight. "Pax," she called, and he turned toward her, his tail doing half circles of delight. "Come on, boy."

He started toward her, then stopped and turned to look behind him back down the beach the way they had just come. Alicia looked beyond the dog and was surprised to see a man coming toward them. All the time she'd been at the cottage, she hadn't seen anyone on the beach at all, and it took her by surprise to see this lone figure strolling near the water.

He stopped, shaded his eyes with his hand and looked out toward the horizon. As his hand fell and his head lifted a bit toward the setting sun, for a split second, with the light not quite as bright and clear as it had been, Alicia felt her whole being clench. For that single heartbeat, she almost thought he was Buck. He was tall and lean, and he held his chin at an angle, the way Buck had when he was thinking.

But as he turned and headed toward her, she knew how much of a fantasy that instant response had been. She saw a stranger walking with a faint limp in his stride as he favored his left leg. And there was no long ebony hair falling straight around a clean-shaven, deeply tanned face. There was brown hair, sun-streaked, short, brushed straight back from a face partially hidden by sunglasses and further hidden by a trimmed dark beard. How could she have been so mistaken?

She looked away, forcing herself to take a deep, cleansing breath, and she stared out to the ocean, her eyes barely seeing the blurred line of the horizon where the water`met the sky. Six months and she still imagined she saw Buck every time she turned and spotted a tall, lean man who moved as if he were in this world completely alone.

She felt Pax by her leg, pushing against her knee, but when she looked down at the dog, she saw he was looking at the stranger, too. She knew she couldn't stay here any longer, and she got to her feet to return to the cottage where she knew she could be alone. As Pax moved away from her, she saw him loping along the sand, but instead of going toward the tide line, he was heading directly for the stranger.

The man stopped and stood very still, apparently watching the dog approach him. As Pax got within five feet, he stopped, cocked his head to one side as if studying the man, then moved slowly toward him, his tail down. When the man dropped to his haunches and reached out to pat Pax, the dog didn't pull away.

Alicia realized how little she understood anything anymore, least of all a dog who made up to no one, going to a complete stranger and letting him pat him. She watched the man stroke the dog's head and neck, and she stared at strong hands ruffling the dark fur.

Shaking her head, she called out to Pax, "Come on, boy. Come here."

Pax turned, his ears lifting in recognition, but he didn't come to her. "This isn't the time to get stubborn," she muttered under her breath. Then she stood and started toward the dog and man.

As she approached, the man stood. The light breeze of the early evening lifted his sun-streaked hair, and the setting sun glinted off his gold-rimmed sunglasses. Casual clothes, cutoff shorts and a navy tank top showed a build that was sinewy and lean.

"I guess he's your dog, isn't he?" His voice faintly hoarse and deep, running oddly over her nerves.

Alicia stopped, the damp sand of the beach under her bare feet, and she reached for Pax's collar to pull him back. "I'm sorry," she said. "He's usually shy around people. He's not the kind to make up to just anyone."

The man glanced down at Pax. "He looks like he's a natural loner, a dog who doesn't need anyone." He looked back at Alicia, his glasses hiding his eyes. Unexpectedly, he held out his hand to her. "James Carlton. I'm staying at a cottage farther down the beach."

Alicia hesitated, then put her hand in his. "Alicia Sullivan," she murmured, and as his fingers closed around hers, she felt heat and strength and a jolting awareness that she'd only felt once before in her life—with Buck.

She drew back quickly, unconsciously rubbing her hand on her shorts to rid herself of the tingling that persisted. Her mind was playing tricks on her, cruel tricks that she couldn't handle. She tugged at Pax by his collar, feeling foolish to have thought she could forget everything just by coming here. Distance and change of location didn't make a speck of difference.

"Nice to meet you," she said, and moved around him to head back down the beach toward the cottage with Pax.

"Alicia?"

She stopped, then turned to see the stranger coming toward her, his limp more pronounced now. She waited for him to get within three feet of her. "Yes?"

He rubbed at his left thigh and shook his head. "I'm not used to this leg yet."

"Are you all right?" she asked.

"I hurt it a while back. They say it's going to heal completely, but it's taking a hell of a long time."

"An accident?"

"A shooting."

"A what?"

"Shooting. You know—guns. Bang. Shooting."

"I'm sorry, I . . ." She didn't know what to say, just that she had to go.

"You like holidays?" he asked, stopping her before she could leave.

"I used to," she admitted.

"I used to know someone who hated them, thought they were just an excuse to get off work."

She felt her heart lurch, and she looked up at the man. Nothing was right. She was still hearing words that Buck had said, as if they hadn't quite died out yet. She felt Pax tug free of her hold on his collar, and she let him go to run toward a flock of sea gulls farther down the beach. She cautiously looked back at the man, certain he'd been talking, but without a clue as to what he'd said. "Excuse me?"

He took a step toward her, diminishing the distance between them to mere inches. "I was just saying about a man who used to scoff at Christmas. I don't think he even believed in the Easter bunny."

She shook her head, the crazy thoughts tumbling in there almost painful for her. "I don't understand," she whispered.

"He hated holidays. He sure wouldn't be here to see fireworks."

Was she imagining this, hallucinating, was he really saying what lovely weather it was, but she was imagining he was talking about Buck? She felt light-headed, and her heart was beating up in her throat. Insanity felt as if it was just a heartbeat away for her. "Did you know...?" She couldn't say the words.

He leaned closer to her and whispered, "Steven Rider is dead."

Horrible hallucinations. The world blurred, and she could barely manage, "What did you say?"

"Steven Rider is dead," he repeated, and she could have sworn he really said those words.

She shook her head, and held her hands out in front of her as if she could ward off the nightmare. "No, don't say that," she gasped, backing up a pace, but he matched her pace and kept within inches of her. "Pax, Pax, we have to go," she called.

She heard him barking behind her, but she couldn't take her eyes off the stranger as he slowly took off his sunglasses. The nightmare exploded when she met a gaze from eyes so blue that it made the deeply colored sky look pale by comparison.

"Oh, God," she gasped, awkwardly backing up, shaking her head so violently from side to side that she felt the sting of her hair across her shoulders. "No. No."

No nightmare before had been this intense, this cruel. She could feel the pain in her body, the band of iron around her lungs. The man came toward her, matching her steps, never letting her get space. She knew she had to run and keep running to get away from the madness. She started to turn, to take flight, but a hand on her upper arm stopped her.

The hold on her felt real, as real as her pain, and as she turned, the man touched her cheek with his free hand, the tips of his fingers caressing her cheek. "Alicia," he whispered. "God, I've missed you."

Buck? She stared at him. The lines weren't quite right, the slant to his eyes, the cheekbones, his jaw. Not quite the same. Yet, if she narrowed her eyes, blurring reality, maybe, just maybe she could see the man she wanted so badly. Maybe she wouldn't have to believe he was dead, that he was lost to her for eternity.

But she couldn't trust in make-believe. Not when she'd have to face reality and start the pain all over again. "No."

His hand stilled on her face. "Oh, yes," he whispered as he cupped her chin.

She felt as if she'd fallen down the rabbit hole and into Wonderland. A place where Buck was. Where he wasn't dead. Where if she looked at him just right, she could see him just inches from her.

And right then she knew that if this was an illusion, so be it. If she was crazy, let her be crazy. All she knew was for this insane moment, she had Buck back again. And she went to him, hugging him so tightly that her arms trembled. She knew that she never wanted sanity again if it meant giving this up.

She held him and sobbed, heart-wrenching sobs that shook her body. And he held her. His heart thundered against her cheek, and she could feel his breathing, his chest moving, the rasp of inhaling and exhaling. And she clung to her fantasy with an intensity that left no room for fact or truth.

She didn't move, terrified if she did he'd dissolve in a puff of smoke, that she'd look and she'd be alone again. She balled the cotton of his shirt in her hands and rubbed her forehead against his chest. "Is it really you, or am I going crazy?"

"Steven Rider's dead. So is Joe Riley, but Buck is right here. Now. With you. Finally. Believe it. I'm here."

She slowly drew back enough to look into his face. "How? I heard on the television that you . . . you were killed. I believed it."

"Everyone was supposed to believe it." He framed her face with his hands, and she could feel an unsteadiness in his touch that was duplicated in her. "Steven Rider had to die, or he would have never been free." He moved his thumbs on her cheeks, brushing at the dampness of her tears, and the sensuous caress played havoc with her already shattered nerves. "I would have never been free to find you again. Shaw would have found me, no matter what. And if you had been with me, you would have died, too." His thumbs stilled on her cheeks. "God, I couldn't have taken that chance."

She drew a shuddering breath. "I would have gone with you . . . anywhere."

"I know. That's why it was so hard to take you to Jon's. I swear to God, I wanted to die when I left you there."

"So did I," she admitted.

"Well, neither one of us died. It was a close call, but—"

"No cigar?" she murmured.

A shadow of a smile played at the corners of his lips. "How about a cigarette?"

She touched her tongue to her lips. "No, no cigarette, either. Just tell me how you got here."

"It's a long story," he said, "and I need a long time to tell you all about it."

"How about forever?" she whispered.

"That was my idea," he said, and his mouth cut off any response she was about to make with a deep, searching kiss that gave vent to all the pain, loneliness and heart-wrenching need of the past six months.

Epilogue

The night was hot and sultry, a perfect Fourth of July, the most perfect Alicia had ever had. Buck was alive. Buck was with her, in the cottage, in the bedroom.

She opened her eyes to deep shadows in the room and saw Buck silhouetted by the windows, naked, looking outside at the second set of fireworks shooting into the night sky.

She didn't say anything for a long while, content to rest on her elbow and just watch him, drinking in his presence. The width of his shoulders, the lean hips, strong legs. The sight made her whole body fill with a desire that threatened to choke her.

"Buck?" she finally said when she felt an almost physical need to touch him again, to feel his heat and strength under her hands, to feel him fill her and be with her.

He turned, his face in shadows. "You're awake?"

"I have been for a while. What are you doing over there?"

"I let Pax out. Then I got to thinking."

"About what?" she asked, wishing she could see him clearly instead of this blurred shadowy image.

"You."

"What about me?"

"Did I tell you that I love you?"

He hadn't ever said the words, but he hadn't needed to. Every touch, every contact had said it to Alicia, but it sounded wonderful to hear it said out loud. "Do you really love me?"

He exhaled, his shoulders moving sharply. "Do I really love you?" He came to her, getting into the bed with her and reaching out for her. "I love you so much that it terrifies me," he said as he hugged her to him. "I don't know what I would have done if Sampson hadn't been able to work things out."

She lay in the shadows with him, her legs tangled with his, her cheek against his heart. He had told her little of how he'd come back, or even why he'd had to leave. "Sampson?"

"My contact. You know about Shaw a.k.a. Sanbourn, and about me testifying against him. Sampson was my protection, the one who set up the safe places to stay. And he's the one who saved my life." He stroked her back with his hand as he spoke.

"When I got back to the cabin, there was a greeting from Shaw, a hit man from Seattle. To make this short and sweet, he was going to kill me, Pax came in, distracted him, and the next thing I knew, I was shot in the leg. I tried to get my gun. He raised the gun again, and Sampson was there. He was minutes behind the hit man. Almost too late, but not quite. The hit man died, and I lived."

His hand stilled, and he rested his chin on her head. "I knew then how right I'd been to get you out of there. Sampson had the place stripped, got me back to testify, and my only happiness was knowing that even though I'd lost you completely, I knew you were safe. No one could link you to me. No one would ever say the name Steven Rider in the same sentence as Alicia Sullivan."

"But you were shot," she whispered as she drew back and touched his thigh, the deceptively small knotted scar just below his hip. "You could have died . . . really died.".

"The wound wasn't major, it just tore up the muscle a bit. And I'm very much alive." He pulled her back to him, not willing to have even inches separating them. "Sampson took care of that. He took care of setting up the fatal accident. He got me a new identity, James Carlton, landscape architect with his own firm in Portland."

"The man sounds like a wonder worker, but is his name really Sampson?"

"No, and I don't have a clue what it really is. All I know is the man's terrific. He kept track of you, what was happening, the fact that you and Jonathan Welsh III were kaput. He even had an idea about how I could be with you and no one would be in danger."

She moved back again and raised herself on one elbow to look down at Buck. The lights from the fireworks outside flashed into the room, playing color and shadows over his face. Off in the distance they heard a dog howl. "Pax?"

"Probably. I doubt that he likes the fireworks, but he wouldn't stay inside."

"A mind of his own," she said. "I hope he knows enough to come back."

"Don't worry. He's a lot like me. I sure as hell know where I belong," Buck said.

She smiled, then the expression faltered. "They changed you, didn't they?"

He gazed up at her. "A nip here, a tuck there. The voice got a bit rougher."

She tapped his chest with one finger. "Some things haven't changed."

"I hope not," he murmured.

"What exactly did this Sampson figure out?"

"That James Carlton could meet Alicia Sullivan, have a whirlwind courtship, and no one would think anything of it."

She touched his nipple and felt it tense under the tip of her finger. "A genius, pure and simple."

"My opinion exactly," he said, and his voice caught as she trailed her finger over the hint of hair that ran down his abdomen. "A genius."

She moved away from him, reached for the side lamp and snapped it on. When she turned back to Buck, he was blinking at the brightness. "Why did you do that?"

She opened the side drawer of the nightstand and turned back to Buck as she opened her hand. The small blue button from his shirt lay in her palm, the only physical proof until now that she had ever met Buck in this world.

He looked at it, then took it between his thumb and forefinger. "What is it?"

"The button from your shirt I wore at the cabin. When I went back, that's all I could find, the only thing that let me know I hadn't imagined all of it."

"You didn't imagine it," he said as he tossed the button into the air and off the bed. "And you don't need that any longer. I'm here."

"Yes, you are." She kissed him quickly and fiercely, then drew back, resting her hand on his chest, feeling his heart beating. Yes, this was very real. "Okay, now let's get this straight. Sampson arranged all of this. He probably put that thing in the computer about this place, didn't he?"

"He asked me where I thought you'd be most likely to go if given an opportunity that was too good to pass up."

"And you told him this cottage?" she asked as she brushed her hand over his stomach.

"I did."

"Then he figured we'd meet as Alicia Sullivan and James Carlton, fall madly in love, and—?"

His hand covered hers, stilling it on his navel. "I can't think if you do that."

"Do you need to think?"

He laughed unsteadily. "I don't know." He let go of her hand and found the curve of her hip with his hand.

"You never finished the statement. We meet, we fall in love and—"

"Madly in love, I think you said." He caressed the swelling of her hip, then moved his hand to her rib cage and under her breast.

"Madly in love, and—?"

"I never thought I'd say this, but we'll get married and live happily ever after."

She looked at him, then began to methodically run her hand over his skin, over his shoulders, his stomach, then his thighs, skimming past the scar, then back to his stomach.

"Alicia?"

"Shhhhh," she breathed. "I'm checking."

"Checking for what?" He sounded as if he couldn't quite catch his breath, and that pleased her. She moved her hand lower and he gasped, "For what?"

"I'm checking for hives." She swept him a look as her hand finally touched the response to her touch that he couldn't hide. "I'm happy to report that there isn't a trace of hives."

He groaned and reached for her, bracketing her waist with his hands and sweeping her on top of him. With a feeling of familiarity that should have only come after years of making love, he slid inside her, and his eyes never left her face as he began to move.

"Happily ever after," he breathed. "Do you believe in that?"

She braced herself over him with her hands pressed to the pillows on either side of his head. "I always have," she whispered.

In a fluid movement, Buck changed places, rolling up until he was over Alicia and looking down at her. "You'll marry me, won't you?"

He moved, and she reached for his hips to keep him still until she could absorb the intensity of the sensations. "Buck, please—"

He stilled, and when she looked into his eyes, she saw a raw emotion that shook her. Vulnerability. The man was scared to death she wasn't going to be with him forever. She reached up, spreading her hands on his chest. "Yes, I'll marry you, Buck, or Steven, or Joe, or even Jim."

He threw back his head and laughed, a sound that thrilled Alicia, and then he sobered and looked down at her. "We can move to Los Angeles in a few months—at least by next year—so you can be close to your sister and her family, and Lydia. I want to meet her. But I'm going to have to be Jim to them."

He began to move slowly, leisurely in her, as if he finally knew he had the rest of his life with her. "I'll be Buck to you. A nickname I've had since childhood. I think that childhood was somewhere back east, but I can't quite remember. I'll have to check my facts with Sampson before I meet them so I don't mess up."

"Don't worry, they'll love you as much as I do."

"As long as it's you and me against the world, I'll die happy," he whispered.

She brushed at his short hair, then touched his beard. "Do you think you could ever grow your hair long again and let it go black? And do you have to wear a beard forever?"

"Give me a few years and no one will remember who Steven Rider was. Then it's long hair and clean-shaven."

She started moving in time with Buck as he stroked her with his strength. "Is this real or am I living in some dream?"

"It's as real as life can get, love." He found her lips with his just as the big finale for the fireworks show went off outside. As he drew back, he said, "And if you don't believe me, I think I just heard rockets go off."

She laughed softly. "So did I. What's next, the earth moving?"

"I don't think there's a chance of an avalanche around here...." His voice trailed out as he stroked her, again and again, until the world began to tremble and move, and Alicia knew the real meaning of two becoming one.

The earthquake on July 4 registered 7.4 on the Richter scale.

*   *   *   *   *

A romantic collection that
will touch your heart....

Mother to with Love '93

Diana Palmer
Debbie Macomber
Judith Duncan

As part of your annual tribute to
motherhood, join three of Silhouette's
best-loved authors as they celebrate the
joy of one of our most precious gifts—
mothers.

Available in May at your favorite retail outlet.

Only from **Silhouette**®

—where passion lives.

Take 4 bestselling love stories FREE

Plus get a FREE surprise gift!

Special Limited-time Offer

Mail to Silhouette Reader Service™

3010 Walden Avenue
P.O. Box 1867
Buffalo, N.Y. 14269-1867

YES! Please send me 4 free Silhouette Intimate Moments® novels and my free surprise gift. Then send me 6 brand-new novels every month, which I will receive months before they appear in bookstores. Bill me at the low price of $2.71* each plus 25¢ delivery and applicable sales tax, if any.* I understand that accepting the books and gift places me under no obligation ever to buy any books. I can always return a shipment and cancel at any time. Even if I never buy another book from Silhouette, the 4 free books and the surprise gift are mine to keep forever.

245 BPA AJCK

Name	(PLEASE PRINT)
Address	Apt No.
City	State	Zip

This offer is limited to one order per household and not valid to present Silhouette Intimate Moments® subscribers. *Terms and prices are subject to change without notice. Sales tax applicable in N.Y.

UMOM-93   © 1990 Harlequin Enterprises Limited

For all those readers who've been looking for something a little bit different, a little bit spooky, let Silhouette Books take you on a journey to the dark side of love with

SILHOUETTE
Shadows™

If you like your romance mixed with a hint of danger, a taste of something eerie and wild, you'll love Shadows. This new line will send a shiver down your spine and make your heart beat faster. It's full of romance and more—and some of your favorite authors will be featured right from the start. Look for our four launch titles wherever books are sold, because you won't want to miss a single one.

THE LAST CAVALIER—Heather Graham Pozzessere
WHO IS DEBORAH?—Elise Title
STRANGER IN THE MIST—Lee Karr
SWAMP SECRETS—Carla Cassidy

After that, look for two books every month, and prepare to tremble with fear—and passion.

SILHOUETTE SHADOWS, coming your way in March.

Silhouette®

SHAD1

INTIMATE MOMENTS®

10TH Anniversary

Celebrate our anniversary with a fabulous collection of firsts....

The first Intimate Moments titles written by three of your favorite authors:

NIGHT MOVES   Heather Graham Pozzessere
LADY OF THE NIGHT Emilie Richards
A STRANGER'S SMILE Kathleen Korbel

Silhouette Intimate Moments is proud to present a FREE hardbound collection of our authors' firsts—titles that you will treasure in the years to come from some of the line's founding members.

This collection will not be sold in retail stores and is available only through this exclusive offer. Look for details in Silhouette Intimate Moments titles available in retail stores in May, June and July.